"Why you kill Walsh, Chuyen? Him not bad fellow for American."

Calmly Chuyen got to his feet, brushing off his knees. "He not dead. Not have time to kill. You not try to stop Chuyen." He heard the rasping sound of Krung pulling his knife out of its sheath.

"You not try to go," countered Krung.

Chuyen growled low in his throat and charged at the smaller man. Krung just stood there. At the last possible moment he stepped to one side and with a deft motion swept his knife toward Chuyen's chin.

Chuyen hurtled past for two or three steps before he ran out of steam. Protectively holding his hand against the side of his neck, he turned to face Krung.

"Now try shaking head, Chuyen."

In the moonlight, Krung could see the bigger man working his mouth, but no words passed his lips, only a strange wheezing noise and a lot of blood. A moment later he toppled forward onto his face.

VIETNAM: GROUND ZERO ™

CAMBODIAN SANCTUARY

ERIC HELM

A GOLD EAGLE BOOK FROM

W✺RLDWIDE ®

TORONTO • NEW YORK • LONDON • PARIS
AMSTERDAM • STOCKHOLM • HAMBURG
ATHENS • MILAN • TOKYO • SYDNEY

First edition April 1989

ISBN 0-373-62717-3

VIETNAM: GROUND ZERO™
CAMBODIAN SANCTUARY

This book is dedicated to the men of the ASA, Special Operations Detachment, Fifth Special Forces, Airborne, and specifically to:

Master Sergeant Albert Fauber
Master Sergeant James Alligood
Master Sergeant Robert Courchaine
Staff Sergeant James Fuller
Staff Sergeant Jimmy B. Williams
Staff Sergeant Tex Herbel
Staff Sergeant James Awana Smith
Sergeant Peter Becola
Sergeant Philip R. Gonzalez

PROLOGUE

Big Orville knew the Army would make him pay for the rifle. What really gripped his ass was the fact that he knew better.

On the very first morning, sitting in the gray bleachers under the hot Panama sun, the wiry, mean-looking Special Forces sergeant teaching jungle warfare had warned the men in his platoon, "Never lay your rifle against a tree and walk away to take a piss. If you do, when you go back to grab your rifle, you'll never find the fucker because every tree in the jungle looks exactly the same as the next."

The class members had tittered nervously among themselves. Just out of advanced infantry training at Fort Benning, Georgia, they were more than a little intimidated by the jungle.

None of them knew anything about jungle and swamp other than the fact the trees and vines were overgrown and a host of nasty creatures lived in the branches and bushes, creatures that wanted to suck your veins dry, sink their fangs into your flesh, pump your blood full of poison. Or put a bullet through your hide.

The black Special Forces sergeant who was pulling jungle warfare detail instead of guard duty at the Fort Gulick ammo dump had continued with his discussion.

"In every class that goes through JOTC there's at least one sorry son of a bitch who loses his rifle, and about every third or fourth class we find a rusty rifle lying against the side of some tree where some other dumb fuckhead laid it back when Christ was a private. Lose your rifle, you get a statement of charges levied against you, you pay for the weapon out of your monthly check and you get an Article Fifteen. And if we ever find the rifle, you don't get a refund. Also, anyone gets bitten by a snake automatically gets an Article Fifteen. If you survive, that is."

Now, one week into the jungle warfare course, PFC Orville Waters, affectionately known as Big O due to his six-foot-six, 240-pound frame, committed a mortal sin. With only an hour to sunset, he placed his M-14 against a palm tree, turned around and walked five or six meters across the gloomily lit jungle floor.

It was the dry season in the rain forest, and the floor of the jungle was overlaid with a thick carpet of dead leaves, flowers and twigs that had fallen from the upper layers of the forest. Brown leaves rustled as Big O's stream of urine washed against them. Finished, he buttoned his fly, hiked his pants, turned around and headed back for his rifle. But he couldn't find the tree. Frantically he called for his buddy. "Slim, give me a hand."

Slim came running, nearly tripping over a cluster of fungi that grew out of a rotting tree trunk. "What's wrong? Bushmaster bite you on the dick?" he asked in a Georgia drawl.

"If he did, you're going to die because I ain't sucking out the poison."

Orville frowned, his face that of a little boy who was tired of being teased. "Very funny. Help me find my gun. If I don't find it before dark—"

"You dumb fuckhead. You didn't."

"Just shut up and help me look for the damned thing."

They enlisted the aid of the rest of the squad and looked for half an hour without luck. Once it was dark, they gave up and set up camp for the night. Surprisingly no one bothered to kid Orville. Everyone's mood was sober. They knew their next stop after Panama was Vietnam. Slim patted him on the shoulder reassuringly, "We'll find it at first light."

Deployed in a crude perimeter defense, the members of the first squad sat with their backs against trees, preparing their evening meal. Orville and Slim had set up their jungle hammocks next to each other.

Slim smacked a can of C-rations against his boot heel, denting the soft metal. Then he placed it next to the low blue flame of a fuel tablet and waited for the spaghetti and meatballs to heat.

"Hey, Big O, how ya doin'?" the Georgian asked.

Big O swatted a swollen mosquito, bloodying the side of his face. "Been thinking about Linda, and I got an erection hard enough to fuck a brick."

"She's quite a looker," Slim recalled. "I wish I could remember what a woman looked like." He picked up a twig and started drawing the shape of a woman in the dirt, first the long curves of her thighs, then big round orbs intended to represent a pair of ample breasts. The stick figure was at best a clumsy rendition of a woman.

"You can't draw for shit," Big O said flatly.

"Sure would help considerable if I could see a naked lady. Hell, my memory's fadin' fast. The drawin' would be a lot more detailed. Maybe you can help me. Do women have one or two breasts?"

Big O mimicked Slim's Southern drawl. "Sure would help if ya'll'd actually ever seen a naked lady."

Slim threw the twig at Orville. "I don't have to be able to draw it to make love to it. Hey, I know. You want to see how well I can draw when I have a model to work from? I'll do an M-14. Gimme yours. I'll use it for reference."

"Fuck you."

"You're welcome."

The conversation between the two friends lapsed into silence. Orville pulled a Polaroid photo out of his shirt pocket and studied it with his flashlight, the red filter casting an eerie glow over the blonde woman's well-endowed figure. She wore the facial expression of a woman who had begrudgingly allowed her picture to be taken in the nude.

When the dent in Slim's tin of spaghetti popped back out from the heat, he pulled the can off the chemical flames, opened it and began to eat from it with a white plastic spoon.

"I heard we get a coupla days off when we finish JOTC," Big O said between mouthfuls of his own meal. "When they cut us loose, I'm heading directly for Colón and the Club Siboney those permanent party guys were talking about. The women down here are supposed to be the most beautiful in the world. I talked to a guy who had one once."

Slim sucked his spoon clean, then stuck it into his pocket. "They must have been puttin' us on. Ain't no woman spreads her legs for only two dollars."

"I don't care if she says two hundred. I'm going to get me one. Or two."

"Those guys at Fort Sherman told me that's how the poor girls down here raise their dowry," one of the other squad members chimed in. They could hear his voice but couldn't see him in the dark.

Slim found the concept appalling. "Do you think their fiancés know?"

Orville was still ogling his girlfriend's naked breasts. "Who cares? I'm getting hornier by the minute. I don't know if I can wait. I may have to go fuck that brick."

"Try my ex-wife some time. Same thing," Slim mumbled to himself.

Orville sighed, kissed the snapshot in the area of Linda's genitals, then stuffed the photo into his pocket. "You know, the more I learn about women, the more I like cars. Just before I got drafted by Uncle Sam, I was looking for a set of wheels. Read in the classifieds where somebody was selling a 1953 Chevy stick shift with a six banger. I called the number and a woman's voice says to come over and look at it. Says she's a widow and all she knows is it's a Chevy and she wants to get rid of her late husband's car. It's in the way, she says. I get over there and this old lady takes me out to the garage, pulls back a tarp and shows me a 1953 Corvette with five hundred miles on the odometer."

Slim's eyes glowed orange-blue in the reflection of the fuel tablets; his drawl got thicker when he was excited. "Why, that's the first year they made 'em. It's a classic."

"Yep. Even before they had the small-block V-8. This one had a hopped-up six-cylinder engine with two one-barrel carbs, a three-quarter cam and headers. Slick as spit on a doorknob."

"How much she want for it?"

"She said a coupla hundred dollars would do, seeing as it was fifteen years old."

Slim emitted a low whistle. "So the old gal didn't know what she had. You buy it or steal it?"

Big O was silent for a while before he answered. "I told her the car was worth a hell of a lot more than a coupla hundred. Told her that if she let me sell it, I'd take forty percent of whatever we made over two hundred bucks. Took me forty-eight hours, and we both made out."

"So what did you do with your share?"

"What do you think? I spent it on—"

Slim broke in. "Pussy."

Big O returned an exasperated grin. "I never paid for it in my life."

"But you just said you were goin' down to the Club Siboney and fuck some whore's brains out with a brick and that you didn't care if she wanted two thousand dollars."

"I never said that. Besides, it's different now."

"So what did you spend the money on, then?"

"A Browning shotgun with a full ventilated rib, twenty-gauge with a modified choke. You wouldn't believe the grain in the walnut. It's almost as nice as the stock on the Kentucky rifle I built, although not as nice as the large-ring Mauser I converted to thirty-ought-six and reblued."

Slim's voice had taken on an exasperated tone. "Man, why are you so hung up on weapons? All you ever talk about are guns, fuckin' and Corvettes, and how big Linda's tits are. Whenever you sit around and get to smokin' and jokin', it always gets around to the same three things over and fuckin' over."

"You got a problem with that?"

"Other than borin' the hell out of me, no."

"Anyway, the money I had left over after I bought the Browning, I stuck in the bank. I been saving all my money. Once I get to Nam and start drawing combat pay, I'll be saving even more bread. By the time I DEROS, I'll have enough saved to buy a brand-new Corvette. A red convertible. With a 327 and dual quads, 4.11 posi rear end and rated at 350 horsepower. It's one fire-breathin' machine. Then I'm going to college. Can you dig it? Me Joe College on the GI bill. You ever see how chicks react to a Vette?"

"Do you mean a veteran or a Corvette?" Slim asked with a note of sarcasm.

"What the fuck do you think, Slim? Anyway, I've seen girls hanging all over Vettes, offering to go down on the guy if he'd let 'em ride around town for five or ten minutes."

"Don't like 'em," said Slim, shaking his head. "Corvettes are plastic. Just like the goddamn M-16. Steel's real. I want me a black Dodge Charger with a big 426 hemi under the hood. Did you see the movie *Bullitt* with Steve McQueen in it? That engine doesn't even wake up until 120 miles an hour. Besides, before you make a down payment on that Vette of yours, you got to pay off that M-14. Remember?"

"Hey, Slim."

"Yeah."

"Let it die, will you . . . ?"

REDS JUMP YANKS AFTER HUEY LANDS—12 KILLED IN BATTLE
by Robin Morrow

Saigon (UPI)—Twelve American infantrymen were killed and 30 wounded in a battle with Vietcong near the Cambodian border, a U.S. spokesman said today. The spokesman said a U.S. Army unit was moving from a helicopter landing zone 20 miles west of Tay Ninh City when firing broke out.

Reinforcements were rushed to the area and the battle continued for over seven hours, with the Vietcong sustaining heavy casualties. The spokesman said 57 dead enemy bodies were found, but because the VC carry away their dead, the actual body count would be much higher.

American soldiers in the fighting reported seeing an armed Caucasian man directing the Vietcong attack on

U.S. Army positions. The official spokesman would neither confirm nor deny the report that the VC are using a former U.S. soldier as a "field marshal."

Unconfirmed sources indicate the man may be an American soldier, PFC Randall Norwood, who has been missing since November 1967 when his convoy was ambushed on Highway One about four miles northwest of Saigon. He was last seen being led away by the Vietcong.

A U.S. Army spokesman refused to comment on why Norwood is considered a deserter and not a POW.

1

MARCH 1, 1968
THE CONTINENTAL
SHELF SAIGON
REPUBLIC OF SOUTH
VIETNAM

The Rose of Saigon was nothing more than an oblong bar-room that reeked of sour beer, vomit and urine, a room crowded with too many tables and chairs and lit by neon Budweiser signs. Despite its ordinariness, the dive was always popular with reporters, who, for the most part, considered covering the Vietnam War to include nothing more adventurous than hanging out at the MACV pressroom from nine to five.

At 1701 hours, like a pack of thirst-crazed jackals, they trotted downtown to the Rose where cigarette smoke hung in a thick cloud like early-morning fog in the valleys of the Central Highlands, geography they would never see first-hand. Safely cocooned in their den where the humid tropical air and the tobacco smoke made it hard to breathe, no one in the press corp complained. They were all too intent on getting drunk. Or laid.

In one dark corner, on the far side away from the jukebox blaring an Animals tune, a man and a pretty woman sat in quiet conversation, seemingly oblivious to the noise around them. One moment the two of them were good-naturedly arguing the finer points of global politics and the next the man's eyes narrowed and his jaw was jutting forward. It was as if the short, wiry CIA operative with black hair plastered against his sunburned forehead had violently switched moods, transforming himself from a charming Ivy Leaguer into a fire-breathing jerk itching for a fight. Jerry Maxwell slapped both hands on the tabletop, jarring the drinks so hard that booze sloshed over the rims and the half-empty glasses very nearly tipped over. The tone of his voice was uncharacteristically menacing. "Robin, I want you to strip off your blouse and bra, climb up on top of this table and sing 'The Ballad of the Green Beret' as loud as you can."

Robin Morrow stared at him in disbelief. Having known Maxwell for over a year, the reporter was used to the man's inappropriate sense of theatrics. She knew that he, like many of his colleagues in the intelligence community, had graduated from an Ivy League college. And while his classmates had all been busy romping in the back seats of '56 Chevys, gaining carnal knowledge, Jerry Maxwell's nose had been buried in his textbooks.

As a result, he had missed out on learning the necessary social skills. Perhaps that fundamental shortcoming explained this, his latest escapade, which she decided not to take seriously. Instead, she threw her head back in laughter and touched his arm. "You're a very funny man, Jerry. I like your offbeat sense of humor. But cool it just this once. All right?"

He turned his head and stared at her hand as if it were a wood tick or some other loathsome creature, then flicked it away and stared straight into her eyes. "I'm serious about this, Robin. Dead serious. Lose the blouse and sing the song, or you'll suffer dire consequences.''

The alluring green-eyed woman didn't respond for a moment as she considered the spectacle of what she would look like perched on top of the rickety table with her ample breasts bared to Saigon, amid all the hoots, hollers and jeers that would be sure to follow from her inebriated colleagues. She shuddered.

Morrow studied her companion's face, trying to divine whether or not his intentions were serious or some sort of perverted gag. ''For God's sake, Maxwell. You know me well enough to know I don't scare easily and that I'm not an exhibitionist. So get your ass back on this planet and let's start having a good time. In short, Jerry. Knock off the bullshit.''

The speech left Maxwell unimpressed. He snickered, ''You're too predictable with your oh-so-touching twinge of false modesty, Robin. Yeah, I know you better than that.'' His voice trembled in anger, ''Yes, you'll do as I say. Lose the blouse. Do it. Now.''

She could see the veins bulging in his forehead and noted that his jaw was clenched as tightly as his fists. She wondered if he had finally succumbed to drugs or alcohol, both addictions an occupational hazard in his line of work, especially in war-torn Saigon. Something had certainly eaten into the depths of his soul.

Maybe it was nothing more than the war and the company intelligence officers were inclined to keep—agents, double agents and valueless weasels who would sell information for gold or drugs. Certainly the strain of constantly looking over your shoulder, of never being able to trust anyone you worked with, of knowing what you yourself did for a living, could corrode a man's integrity like nothing else could.

Maxwell leaned back in his chair, removed his right hand from the tabletop and slipped it under his jacket.

"So you think you won't have to do it, huh? Your simple-minded female strategy is to wait me out. I expected you'd need some further motivation." His scowl turned into an evil sneer, his facial expression that of a man who knew a secret. "Time to escalate. I trust you'll do my bidding, my dear little Robin, because my hand is resting on the pistol grip of a .357 Magnum. And if you don't climb up on the table and do exactly as I say, when I say, I'm going to draw this little six-shooter and, in front of God and country and the local Fourth Estate, accelerate a bullet right through the middle of your pretty little forehead."

Morrow looked into his eyes and didn't like what she saw. Feeling a chill in the hollow of her stomach, she squirmed in her chair and blurted, "Surely you're not serious." She was beginning to fear, however, that he was.

Maxwell blinked. "I'm dead serious." With his free hand he began to pat the tabletop in a steady rhythm, the tempo coming faster and faster. "Come on, Robin, show me your boobs, sing me a song." He paused a moment before going on to say, "Or make your peace with your god."

Frowning, she placed a hand on the top button of her white blouse and undid it. She started to reach for the next button, which would expose her cleavage nearly to her belly button, but she paused, folded her arms across her chest and leaned across the table until her nose was barely an inch away from Maxwell's. "Okay, Jerry, I'm calling your bluff. Shoot me." She stared directly into his eyes.

He snickered. "You'll be dead, Robin. I shoot to kill. I won't hesitate for a minute."

Morrow's face took on a serious expression. "You do what you have to, Jerry. And Mack Gerber and Tony Fetterman will do whatever it is they feel compelled to. I predict they'll shoot you, buster, and your dead body will end up lying right beside mine."

He didn't have an answer for that one. The stalemate lasted for thirty seconds as Maxwell tried to stare down Morrow while she just sat there and stared back, unblinking. Finally she broke the impasse. "Okay, Jerry, you've made your point. Sort of. Whatever it is. What's the purpose of this asinine charade you've been boring me with?"

Maxwell's hand came out from under his coat. He showed her his empty palms, then he took a healthy swig of whiskey and water. "I apologize for the strong-arm tactics." He waved his hand, as if doing so would dispel the tension of what had just occurred. "I wanted to illustrate to you in a very dramatic way the value of a secret weapon. Show, don't tell. You see, as long as it's secret, a weapon is for all intents and purposes as useless as an empty gun. For a secret weapon to be truly effective, not only does the other side have to know you've got it, they've absolutely got to know you won't hesitate to use it."

Robin Morrow looked across the table at her companion as if he were crazy. "What do you mean a secret weapon is totally useless? How can that be? And if that's the case, then why do Federal judges lock people in prison for giving away state secrets? In fact, why do we even bother with state secrets?"

"I just showed you," Maxwell said, drumming his fingers impatiently on the tabletop. He had stressed the word *showed*. "When I told you to climb up onto the table, you weren't intimidated by me in the least." He shrugged. "A little outraged, maybe. But in spite of the fact that I had a secret weapon in my shoulder holster, you didn't budge, mainly because I hadn't said anything about a gun yet. You didn't even know I had one. But once you found out that I had a secret weapon, the revolver, and you were forced to consider the possibility that I might use it, you took me a hell of a lot more seriously. Listen, Robin, if a stranger pulled that little routine on you in a dark alley, I guarantee you would have danced for him and done anything else he wanted. Anything.''

Unimpressed by his explanation, Morrow picked up her glass and took a sip of her drink. ''You didn't answer my question. If all this is true, the value of a secret weapon and all that, then why do they make traitors stand trial and then send them to prison for very long periods of time?''

He chuckled. ''You don't understand. It's all part of the game. First consideration. It's good business to leak certain kinds of information to enemy agents. The Reds do it. We do it. Happens all the time. Some unlucky pawns even get killed in the process.'' He laughed. ''Back when Khrushchev was still running the Soviet Union he once trembled in front of a group of Japanese newspapermen and told them, 'Not far from here in a Moscow suburb I saw something so terrible that I do not dare talk about it. I am afraid of what scientists carry with them. Peace must be maintained at all costs. Otherwise we are all dead, the world lost.' Don't you think old Nikita knew how to play the game?''

Robin Morrow continued to stare at Maxwell, now convinced he had gone mad. Maxwell ignored the look as he continued with his story. ''In spite of the peasantlike media image he milked for all it was worth, Nikita understood the deal. You have to make it look good. In a chess game you need pawns on the board just as much as you do rooks and knights. Nikita knew how to work the press like a chess master.''

Morrow narrowed her eyes. Her voice was quiet and controlled. ''Jerry, what would you have done if I had started to take off my blouse. Would you have waited until I showed you my breasts before you called off the game? At what point would you have stopped the goddamn silliness?''

"Guess it would have depended on how well you sang. No, seriously, I don't think I want to answer that question." He smiled conspiratorially, reaching across the table to caress the back of her hand. "Let me keep the answer to your question my little secret."

She pulled her hand away. "Listen, Jerry, you've been more than a little weird lately. I'm not entirely sure I want to go on this little jaunt into Cambodia with you, exclusive story or not." She pointed an accusing finger at his nose. "If you're going weird on me, you're not an asset, you're a liability. I like you fine, Jerry. I appreciate you using your good office to set up this interview with the American deserter." She shook her head. "But I don't know about you anymore. Tell me I'm wrong, Jerry. Tell me you're not losing control. Make me believe. Otherwise the trip is canceled."

"Don't try to bullshit me, Robin. I know you want this story. It's too good to pass up. American GI deserts to team up with the NVA, runs with them for two years, and now he wants to tell his side of the story to the American people, to the bleeding heart liberals. No, don't try to bullshit a bullshitter. You'd tag along on this one even if I was a drug-addicted ax murderer. Ten to one says this guy's tired of living in the jungle, wants to come home and figures he can pave the way with newsprint. You'll tag along."

THE NEXT MORNING Morrow and Maxwell met their ride at Hotel Three at Tan Son Nhut. Morrow knew the location of the helipad well from her frequent forays into the bush with Special Forces Captain MacKenzie K. Gerber. But this time, instead of an OD-painted Huey, she climbed into the cargo compartment of an Air America helicopter, an ominous-looking Bell UH-1D painted flat black and without markings, insignia or identification of any kind. The aircraft was sterile, meaning it couldn't be associated with any nation or army. In short, it didn't exist.

During her first days in Vietnam, Morrow had considered such black-mask paint jobs to be nothing more than a senseless charade. She reasoned that even a Communist could figure out any helicopter beating the air over North Vietnam or Cambodia or Laos could only be American. Who else would try to be sneaky about it? In time she realized stealth wasn't even the point of the exercise. It didn't matter who it belonged to or who knew it.

What did matter was the fact that without markings to identify its origins, a front-page photo of the aircraft published in *Pravda* or any other Communist newspaper wouldn't have quite the impact it would if the Stars and Bars were painted across the fuselage in the good old red, white and blue. In essence, without OD paint and insignia, it was the Communists' word against that of the U.S. It was all a game. The kind of play that excited the likes of Jerry Maxwell.

And now on her way to Cambodia, Morrow sat on a troop seat in the clandestine Huey's cargo compartment, her camera bag on the floor between her ankles. Without thinking she snagged and secured the oversize seat belt as she had done innumerable times before; the buckle was so large that it made her feel as if she were sitting on a giant's chair.

A scowling redheaded man dressed in the Air America uniform of aviator, sunglasses, gray trousers and white shirt climbed into the cargo compartment and squatted on his haunches between Morrow and Maxwell. That was when Morrow also noticed he was wearing rattlesnake cowboy boots and that his footwear matched his temperament. His face was contorted by either rage or disgust; she wasn't sure which. She wondered what his problem was, whether it could be attributed to the heat, the humidity or simply a chronic personality disorder. The latter would make him a shoo-in for agency work, she thought.

Crouched next to Maxwell, the pilot began a brief lecture. "Cambodia, huh? Listen, buddy, we got better things to do than to run you spooks out into the boonies so you can make points with round-eyed women." He looked directly at Morrow, holding the gaze long enough for her to register his disgust of her kind, then he turned back to face Maxwell.

The agent shook his head. "This flight is mission-essential. And I'm not having any trouble with round-eyed secretaries. This trip is pure business. 'Sides, what's got you on edge, Mickey? Miss your nap time?"

The pilot turned his head and spit onto the floor of the cargo compartment. "Naw. Nothing like woman trouble. I just don't like being diverted. I was supposed to be in Hong Kong tonight. Now we'll never make the flight."

"There's always tomorrow."

The pilot aggressively waggled a finger in Maxwell's face. "No. You don't understand. This is business. You got your business, I got mine." He gave a subtle nod in the direction of the cargo compartment deck where an OD tarpaulin covered a vague shape.

"Oh," said Maxwell, the tone of his voice registering the fact that he understood the pilot's situation.

Mickey slapped his knees and stood. "So long as we understand each other." Grumbling to himself, he stepped forward into the cockpit.

Morrow elbowed Maxwell in the ribs. "What's under that tarp?" she asked. The two of them stared at the lump buried under a spread of OD canvas.

The rotors began to spin as the flight crew started the turbine. Soon they'd be on their way into Cambodia where they were to rendezvous with the American deserter. Again she asked Maxwell, "What's under the tarp?"

Maxwell shrugged noncommittally. "Whatever you want it to be."

"I bet it's gold," she said in an excited voice. "Probably payment by the U.S. government for pulling downed pilots out of the jungle. Your buddy Mickey's on his way to sell it on the black market in Hong Kong or Macau. Everybody knows they pay Air America in gold for behind-the-lines flights. No big deal."

Maxwell's face registered a nervous grin. "You don't want to know what's under there. Trust me on this one. You really don't." And then he turned away from the bulge in the tarp, looked out the cargo compartment doorway and watched the ground pull away as they took off.

Morrow smiled. "Must be a secret weapon, huh?" she yelled to him over the noise of the turbines and thrashing rotor.

Her well-timed sarcasm hit home. Maxwell's grin faded.

After they took off and gained altitude, Maxwell studied the broad expanse of the Air Force complex at Tan Son Nhut, with dozens of sandbagged revetments designed to protect planes from sappers, and runways busy with camouflage-painted F-4 Phantoms taking off and landing.

Morrow just sat there looking at the tarp, wondering what secrets it concealed. Obviously the lump was some kind of contraband, but the question was what kind of booty? Thai stick, opium, marijuana? Morrow didn't think the CIA had any more morality than the *cao boi* of Saigon's streets did. Or the NVA, who routinely sold heroin to U.S. soldiers in order to pay for weapons and ammunition that would be used to kill other U.S. soldiers.

Mind wandering, she sat there facing the cargo compartment door, watching the scenery along Highway One roll past below them. A sprinkling of Lambrettas, ox carts, Army jeeps and trucks seemed to crawl along the paved two-lane road. She could also see where all the trees had been knocked down for a 150 feet on either side of the thoroughfare. In spite of the tranquil view, she knew that convoy commanders who didn't follow SOP to the letter were regularly ambushed and wiped out by VC raiding parties.

Finally, tired of studying the scenery, her curiosity got the better of her and she unfastened her seat belt and scooted down the row of seats until she was directly over the tarp. Grasping the corner of the canvas, she paused for a moment and predicted that she'd unveil the unmistakable sparkle of a dozen gold bars. Instead, when she lifted the canvas she saw a simple burlap bag. Then it moved. She reached a hand toward it, intent on opening it and peeking inside.

Suddenly she felt a hand roughly clasp her shoulder. Maxwell's voice boomed above the roar of the engine, "Don't touch it. It's Sam the Sham, Mickey's legendary rattlesnake."

In shock, she dropped the canvas and muttered, "Christ! This war gets stranger every day." Then she looked forward in the direction of the pilots. Neither Mickey nor his Peter pilot had seen her lift the canvas. That knowledge relieved her somewhat.

"Like I said before," shouted Maxwell over the sound of the popping rotors, "You don't want to know. In fact, you didn't even see it. It isn't there." He looked surprisingly calm and contented, almost as if he were seated in a church pew among a gaggle of Methodists for Sunday services instead of on his way to illegally enter Cambodia.

The two of them returned to their seats and strapped themselves in. Morrow remained puzzled, thinking it didn't make sense. She didn't understand why transporting a snake was such a big secret; nevertheless, she decided to go along with Maxwell's wishes. Without uttering a word, she pantomimed the three monkeys: hear no evil, see no evil, speak no evil.

Maxwell seemed pleased. He smiled, knowing she understood. Or so it seemed. He closed his eyes, rested his head against the Huey's bulkhead and drifted off into a catnap. Conserve energy, he thought. They might need it in the next twenty-four hours.

2

AN UNNAMED VILLAGE
CAMBODIA

Sometime after crossing the border into Cambodia near the
Angel's Wing, the Air America Huey made a course change,
toward the north, skirting the eastern edges of Svay Rieng
and Phumi Cham. They had made a big loop until they were
now directly west of Tay Ninh. Without warning, the helicopter started losing altitude near a crossroad village located
along the stretch of highway that ran from Saigon to Phnom
Penh.

"This must be the place!" Maxwell shouted above the
noise of the engines. He studied the scene. Along the shoulder of the asphalt was a dirt pathway worn into a sharp-sided
rut by generation after generation of stoop-shouldered peas-
ants trudging off to work the rice paddies. Flanking Highway One, a long line of broad-leafed trees provided occasional
patches of shade. Morrow gazed at the dry rice paddies
stretching off to the horizon, separated by grassy dikes and
an occasional grove of coconut palms. A bridge with a col-
lapsed span and great slabs of concrete slanted steeply toward the muddy waters beneath.

As they came in low over the village, Morrow noticed the marketplace was alive with men and women selling chickens, produce and herbal remedies. Off to one side stood a circle of cheering men, hands raised over their heads, some fists clenching wads of paper currency. To a man they were so intent on their own activities that no one looked up at the American helicopter.

From his area studies, Maxwell knew the town's population was about two thousand and that the principal industry was the rice mill, owned by the mayor, who was suspected of being a Communist. But such details didn't matter right now; they were interested in the American deserter who had decided he wanted to come in from the heat.

Setting down a hundred yards away from the marketplace, the Huey kicked up a cloud of red dust. Morrow and Maxwell hopped out of the cargo compartment and expected to turn around and see the sunglass-wearing Mickey waving as he lifted off, hell-bent for his rendezvous in Hong Kong. Instead, the pilot had killed the turbine, and before the rotors had stopped spinning, he'd climbed out of the cockpit, thrown back the canvas and grabbed his contraband gunnysack. Like a man who knew exactly where he was going and what he was doing, he trotted off to join the crowd of cheering men.

Maxwell took off after him, calling back to Morrow. "Come on. You gotta see this."

His enthusiasm puzzled her as she began to follow him. Not wanting to get separated in the crowd, she caught up with him, and the two of them elbowed their way into the throng of men. Momentarily Morrow recoiled at the overpowering stench of sour body odor commingling with beery breath, but she soon forgot about the stink once she saw what the men were watching.

In the middle of the clearing, separated by a few feet, were a mongoose and a cobra. Maxwell pointed at the snake. "That's a little one, about a six- to ten-footer. Full-grown king cobras can grow up to eighteen feet long."

The furry little black-and-buff mongoose hissed and circled back and forth in front of the serpent, intentionally trying to provoke it into an attack. The dark brown cobra lay coiled, lazily raising its head above its coils just enough to follow the mongoose's movements. Maxwell added, "Watch the cobra. Nothing much will happen until it rises up to strike."

Choosing the moment, the cobra rose up into an S pattern and started to inflate its hood. Without warning it struck, but the mongoose deftly sidestepped the lunge. The snake recoiled and the mongoose was soon back to the business of teasing and taunting.

Morrow found herself comparing the mismatch of the tiny mammal and the big serpent to that of a bantam-weight amateur boxer trying to bully the heavyweight champion of the world. The cobra struck again, and once more the agile mongoose darted out of the way in time. The cobra struck again and again, but each time the mongoose used its fancy footwork to avoid sudden death.

Beginning to tire after several strikes, the cobra struck once more, extending its body to the limit as it fell to the ground. Faster than the snake could recoil, the mongoose leaped into the air and landed on the back of the snake's neck, sinking its fangs into the serpent's head and crushing the skull. Watching the furry beast begin to devour the head, Morrow thought she could hear the sound of bones crunching.

The winners and losers were easy to spot as frowning men counted out paper currency and begrudgingly handed it over to smiling men. The man who owned the mongoose smiled broadest of them all as his partner counted the winnings.

Behind them a wiry Cambodian grabbed the dead cobra by the tail and started dragging the carcass off toward the marketplace, leaving blood and brains trailing in the sand behind him.

Even though the serpent had lost the contest, the dried skin would be worth plenty of money to wealthy Westerners who liked to strut around honky-tonks in exotic cowboy boots. And among Cambodians and other Southeast Asians, the meat was considered a rare delicacy by those elite households that liked to partake in a feast of snakes. Furthermore, shamans prized the medicinal and aphrodisiacal powers of the venom and fangs.

Maxwell and Morrow looked on as Mickey approached the man who owned the mongoose. The two of them jabbered back and forth for a couple of minutes. Then a stern-faced Mickey walked to the bloody sand where the cobra had been defeated, carefully set the gunnysack on the ground and untied the loop of twine that held it shut. With a practiced motion he dumped his rattlesnake. Instantly Sam the Sham was alert, circling and thrashing his fat, long body on the ground, hissing, flicking his tongue, obviously outraged at having been unceremoniously dumped on scalding hot and dusty ground under the tropical sun.

Besides, he was hungry; days had passed since he had been fed his last rat. As Sam the Sham slithered across the sand, the crowd chattered and pointed at the strange glazed diamondback pattern on his skin. And when the snake moved too close to them, the crowd showed respect by backpedaling in unison to get out of the way. Finally they placed the mongoose on the ground.

The rattlesnake stopped cold, looked at the mongoose and hissed once. The mongoose responded with its twittering voice, then started circling back and forth, moving closer and closer to the snake. The serpent responded to the challenge by vibrating his tail.

Morrow stood there transfixed. Maxwell yawned. Morrow said, "My God, Jerry, how can you be bored by all this? Those two creatures are going to try to kill each other. It's life or death."

Maxwell shrugged. "Mickey's snake is going to win. He always does. No contest."

"How can you be so certain?"

"Just wait. Just watch. You'll see soon enough. You want to put some money on it?"

She didn't have time to answer. The mongoose had been creeping closer and closer, but unlike the previous encounter with the cobra, this time the rodent appeared confused and disoriented. The animal kept waiting and waiting for the rattler to loom up into an S pattern and inflate his hood. Then, without warning, with the mongoose only a few feet away from his intended victim, the rattlesnake struck out, sinking sharp fangs into the mongoose's flanks. The force of the strike bowled the creature over. Then the snake curled up into a protective curl. The mongoose quivered for a moment and then just lay there motionless on the ground with its eyes open.

"Poor little creature," said Morrow. "Horrible way to die."

Maxwell stared at her. "He didn't feel a thing."

Hands on her hips, she snapped, "Is that so? One time I was out on patrol with Gerber and I stepped on a baby mamba. The sole of my boot caught it right behind the head, and it still managed to strike at me. The fangs didn't penetrate the leather, but it still felt as if someone had smacked me with a ballpeen hammer. Bruised my big toe black and blue. Now go ahead, bright guy, and tell me that little mongoose didn't feel any pain."

At first the crowd oohed and awed at the outcome of the mongoose versus cobra match, but soon they started chattering angrily among themselves as lost wagers were paid off and the winners began good-natured ribbing.

In the middle of it all, a young boy with a mischievous expression on his face came jogging out of the crowd. All of the men jeered and catcalled, knowing exactly what the youth was up to. Without missing a step, he expertly place-kicked the dead mongoose so that it came down directly in front of Sam the Sham. Out of fear and anger, the tormented serpent struck again, striking his prey so hard this time that the mongoose rolled at least three yards before it stopped. By then Mickey had the neck of the gunnysack open wide and was concentrating on gathering up his rattlesnake.

"Like I said," Maxwell told Morrow, "his rattlesnake always wins. It isn't even a fair contest. Notice how the mongoose seemed lost? He was waiting for Sam to rise up like the cobra and inflate his hood. He never did because diamondbacks don't screw around with all that posturing and chest-beating. They never threaten. They just strike. It isn't even a fair contest. The mongoose plays by one set of rules, Sam the Sham by another. I don't think the indigenous population will ever figure it out, and until they do, Mickey will keep making *beaucoup* money. Especially in Hong Kong. And now you know the rest of the story." Maxwell checked his wristwatch, then turned away from the crowd and started walking toward the town proper. "Come on, let's catch our ride. He'll be here in exactly five minutes."

IT WAS DARK, and it seemed evident to Robin Morrow that their carefully planned schedule was shot to pieces. Back in Saigon, Maxwell had indicated to Morrow that a car was supposed to pick them up at the village and drive them to the rendezvous site where the interview with the deserter was supposed to take place. But Mickey and his flight crew had taken off in the Air America helicopter hours ago.

The mongoose-and-cobra fight crowds had long since dispersed, and nothing in the village seemed to be moving except for squadrons of pesky flies and blood-sucking mosquitoes.

Even late into the day the tropical sun burned hot. Rivulets of sweat rolled down Maxwell's tired face. "Christ, it's hot," he said.

Morrow nodded, then addressed the real issue. "Your contact is late."

Maxwell responded impatiently. "So much for the Cambodian notion of station time," he said sarcastically as he angrily swatted the side of his face.

Chuyen, Maxwell's link with the deserter, had told them they were to wait at the rice mill. They had had no trouble locating the mill, and had been sitting in the shade with their backs against the wall. Then, weary of waiting for the ride that might never show, Maxwell and Morrow started walking toward the cluster of thatched huts down the road. The village seemed strangely deserted. No babies cried for their mothers, no children played, no dogs barked around the houses.

"It's too quiet. I don't like it," said Maxwell. "I don't like this at all."

Ten paces away from a hut sporting a red-and-white Coca-Cola sign that glinted in the sunlight, a man in a pale blue sport shirt stepped out of the doorway and pointed an AK-47 at their chests. Morrow recognized him from earlier in the afternoon. He had been standing in the crowd, watching the spectacle, but not really participating.

Not needing any more prompting than the sight of the man's weapon, Maxwell quickly brought his hands up.

Without moving his lips or teeth, he whispered to Morrow, "VC."

"No shit," murmured Morrow.

The gunman barked something in Vietnamese. When the response from the two Americans was puzzlement, he tried English. "Who are you?"

"I'm Robin Morrow. This is Jerry Maxwell. We're journalists. We're not soldiers."

Another young Vietnamese came out of the hut wearing a U.S. Army boonie hat and carrying an M-16 rifle. He angrily pointed a finger at Morrow. "You not journalist. You agents of CIA." He took a step toward Maxwell and roughly shoved him to the ground. He glowered at Morrow. "Turn around. You come Cambodia in CIA helicopter." He pointed his rifle menacingly at her.

Morrow visibly paled. Slowly, deliberately, she put her hands up. "We don't want to turn around. We're afraid you'll kill us." She stared at the second man's face, noticing he only had one eye, the empty socket was red, puckered and oozing with infection. Oh, shit, thought Morrow, he had probably lost the eyeball in some battle with American troops. She knew the depth of hatred an injury like his could generate. It would be enough that she was American; she didn't even have to be a combatant to draw his wrath.

The VC with the AK raised his eyebrows and looked at his one-eyed buddy. They both smiled and looked at Morrow as if she had just squatted on her haunches and howled at the moon. "You crazy," he told Morrow. "We not shoot you. You turn around and march down road with hands over head."

The one-eyed man took his turn. "Not be afraid," he said, wagging a finger. "We capture man. We never kill. War not to kill but to win cause. Uncle Ho believe bad people misled. Bad Americans not understand. We no like kill American soldiers. They misled, not understand. Not right thinking. We capture, educate. No more bad.''

Yeah, right, thought Maxwell. No like kill GIs, my gullible ass. Then where did you get that M-16, asshole.

The four of them started walking Indian file in the humid evening heat, covering what seemed to be ten klicks of bad road. Maxwell estimated an hour had passed, though, locating them about three miles away from the hut. He had determined that if they were to escape they would need to know where the hell they were. Besides, counting paces helped pass the time and kept him from worrying about whatever fate might befall them. He hoped they wouldn't be blindfolded, but ruled that out as impractical. If the captives couldn't see, they'd stumble and fall every few feet, holding the VC back.

Maxwell nervously entertained visions of being marched to the side of a shallow grave where they would be shot to death and their bodies dumped in. He corrected himself. No, they'd probably rape Morrow first and make him watch. Then kill me.

Plodding along behind him, Morrow was in better spirits, feeling less nervous now that they were on the move. After all, they had survived the crucial first few moments. It seemed a logical conclusion that all she had to do was convince the VC that they, or at least she, was a newspaper correspondent and not a CIA operative. If she could pull that off, they'd probably get out of the jam. And she'd have one hell of a story, a story other Saigon correspondents would kill for.

She stared at the back of Maxwell's head as they walked along, considering the fact that while it would be a simple task to verify who she was, Maxwell might very well be in deep trouble.

3

APRIL 1, 1968
OPERATIONS BUNKER
CAMP A-555 FIFTH
SPECIAL FORCES
(AIRBORNE) COMPOUND
REPUBLIC OF SOUTH
VIETNAM

Chuyen was a double agent. At least that was the raised-eyebrow suspicion of the S-2 types assigned to the Fifth Special Forces Group, Airborne, stationed in Nha Trang. But even though Chuyen was only suspected of being a double agent, Special Forces Captain MacKenzie K. Gerber intuitively knew it was true as clearly as he knew Ho Chi Minh was a Communist.

Gerber didn't like working with traitors, but working with both suspected and proven traitors was one of the vagaries of war. A smart officer would use all of his assets no matter how distasteful the liaison might be. As long as the Vietnamese-born Chinese didn't know the Americans were onto his charade, he could be used against his own unsuspecting bosses back in Hanoi.

And now in the midst of a debriefing, Gerber and Chuyen were huddled over a map of Cambodia. Just returned from a behind-the-lines intelligence gathering mission, Chuyen babbled away in broken English, pointing out NVA and Vietcong troop movements he had allegedly observed along stretches of the Ho Chi Minh Trail where it skirted the Cambodian-South Vietnamese border north of Camp A-555.

Chuyen had ostensibly been inside the Cambodian sanctuary, seventy-five miles northwest of Saigon, where the gray defoliated jungle gave way to lush green foliage and where MACV intelligence estimates had placed at least four NVA divisions and thousands of VC. Think-tank strategists commonly believed one of the keys to the Communists' staying power was this Cambodian sanctuary, the haven from which they were able to infiltrate into South Vietnam with supplies or to launch a general offensive.

In great detail Chuyen recounted enemy troop strength and described the equipment they had been carrying; he did so to the point of estimating exactly how many rounds of small-arms ammunition each man had lugged southward.

Throughout Chuyen's animated recitation of facts and figures, Gerber wondered how much of the intelligence data the man relayed was utter truth and how much was disinformation intended to befuddle American war strategy. The Green Beret captain knew double agents would sprinkle bits of fact among the fabrications in order to make the overall picture appear as solid as steel-reinforced concrete.

Gerber feigned dedicated interest, stroking his chin, nodding attentively and asking insightful questions when he deemed it appropriate. All the while he was really thinking, Chuyen, you lying, two-faced, Communist bastard. Carefully maintaining the charade, he chose that moment to smile approvingly at the double agent.

"You've done very well, Chuyen. I'm pleased with your results."

Then Chuyen dropped the bomb. "Oh, I know where journalist Morrow being held."

Gerber's stomach felt like ice. Frantically he hoped his facial expression didn't betray his inward twinge of emotion. You dirty bastard, he thought. You just waited with that little item to watch me squirm. It had been days since his girlfriend had disappeared in Cambodia without a trace. There hadn't been a word since the Air America helicopter had let them out. Until now.

Chuyen went on. "She and Maxwell alive. Prisoners of North Vietnamese army." The black-haired man jabbed a short, stubby finger at the map, roughly approximating the Cambodian border area he had just left. "You like, I take you right to them. No problem."

Gerber worked hard to keep the timbre of his voice nonchalant. "Where are they? Show me their exact location on the map. I want grid coordinates to plug in." He was frustrated enough that he felt the urge to grab the shaggy-haired Chuyen and shake him in spite of the fact that the Chinese stood a full head taller than he. The lankily built Chuyen was tall for a Caucasian, let alone an Oriental.

The double agent shook his head. "No can do. They all time on move. NVA sleep different place every night. Sometime village, sometime jungle. We must go province. I sneak around find out. We ambush Charlie, rescue you friends real good. You and Fetterman come with me Cambodia. Just over border, two, three klicks. Get you girlfriend Morrow. Bring her back to Saigon. You happy. She happy." He thumped his own skinny chest. "Chuyen happy."

For fifteen minutes Gerber went around and around with Chuyen, quizzing him about how he knew where Robin Morrow and Jerry Maxwell were being held and by whom.

Chuyen betrayed just enough to hold his interest, yet never yielding enough solid information for him to act on his own. It was all wrapped up in a neat little package and tied in a pretty red bow. He wouldn't tell where they were prisoners, and instead they had to go in and get them. Nice. Very nice, mused Gerber.

Finally, convinced he had heard all Chuyen was going to reveal, Gerber decided to dismiss him. Besides, he needed time to sift through and interpret the information, or misinformation, he had just been handed.

On the way out the door Chuyen paused to tell him he was looking forward to deploying again in Cambodia because he hated the NVA so much. He called out to Captain Gerber, "What you call forty-nine VC floating face down in Mekong?"

"I don't know, Chuyen. What do you call forty-nine VC floating facedown?"

"A beginning."

Green Beret Captain MacKenzie K. Gerber was on the promotion list for major, and with this, his second tour of duty in Vietnam, it was likely to go through before he DEROSed to the World. That was, he reflected, unless he got himself killed on a direct-action mission behind enemy lines, on a mission precisely like the one Chuyen was proposing.

There was a knock on the door, and without waiting for an invitation to enter, Master Sergeant Anthony B. Fetterman strolled in. Hooking a thumb over his shoulder, he said, "Saw Chuyen leave and knew you'd want to hash over whatever intel he picked up. You still think he's turned on us?"

"Surer than I was before he set foot in here an hour ago," Gerber replied. "He just told me Robin's alive, and he knows where she is."

Fetterman whistled. "Quite a coincidence that our man would be privy to information like that. How did he happen to pick it up?"

"Oh, this guy is one clever fellow. He used the language barrier to his advantage, kowtowing and begging off that he doesn't quite understand my question or doesn't know how to translate what he knows from Chinese into English." Gerber slammed his fist on the desk. "I'd like to cut his tongue out with a rusty pocket knife."

By now Gerber had hunched over the map, and Fetterman had followed his lead. Gerber swept his fingers along the Cambodian frontier, west of Tay Ninh Province.

"He says she's been captured by the NVA and they're on the move in here, never staying put."

Fetterman stood up, then swore a blue streak. "Let me guess, he thinks we ought to go in after her...."

Gerber seemed lost in his own thoughts. "I didn't like it from the start. Didn't like her tagging along with Maxwell. Didn't like her going to Cambodia. And I sure as hell didn't like Chuyen conveniently coming up with information on her whereabouts."

"You already know what I'm going to say," Fetterman said. "Group says we can't trust him. Let's extend that possibility. He may know where she is and is trying to lure us into Cambodia so he can murder us." He shrugged. "On the other hand, maybe he really doesn't know where she is, but is trying to lure us behind the lines in order to murder us."

"There's only one point I disagree with you on, Master Sergeant."

"Oh, what's that?"

"Simple. U.S. Army personnel aren't murdered. They're killed in action."

"There's an important issue involved here. We can't mount a clandestine mission into Cambodia with the express purpose of rescuing Robin, even if she is your girl-friend. As far as Pentagon West and our brothers at Nha Trang see it, she's just another U.S. citizen who's blundered into an untenable situation."

Gerber agreed wholeheartedly. "I've already thought of that. On the other hand, this whole setup reeks of opportunity to smoke out Chuyen and prove his allegiance. The proverbial two birds with one stone."

"There is another possibility I think we should consider," said Fetterman. His mood had turned sober.

"Yeah, Tony. I already know what you're going to say. Not only is there a price on our heads, just like there is for any SFer, but capturing us specifically would hold a special delight for the enemy. Their propaganda specialists would whoop and holler in delight if we bit the dust."

"So you agree with my basic premise that the Hanoi think tank probably set up Robin and Maxwell in order to lure us into Cambodia? And you don't really think I'm paranoid?"

"Like the man said, even paranoiacs have enemies. It works for me. It would be quite a coup for Giap's guys."

"So what do we know about Chuyen?" Fetterman asked. "What's the unofficial scoop?"

Gerber walked over to a gray combination-lock filing cabinet, retrieved a standard 201 personnel file folder from the top drawer and began to thumb through the sheaves of paper inside.

"Chuyen is one of Chinese ancestry, born and reared in Cholon, which, as you know, is Saigon's Chinatown. Been working with S-2 out of Nha Trang for two years, specializing in infiltrating Cambodia and mixing in with the locals, keeping his eyes and ears open. He was hot as hell for a while. Then about six months ago the pattern changed for no apparent reason. On close examination we started finding holes in the intel he was bringing in. Other stuff that did prove out, he shouldn't have been able to bring in.''

Fetterman offered a string of possibilities. "Maybe he's being blackmailed, or owes big money. He's Chinese. Maybe he's got uncles or cousins behind the bamboo curtain and the Communists got word to him that either he cooperates or heads will roll. Wouldn't be the first time.''

"If he's turned, I don't care why. His personal problems don't matter to me. Right now I'm most concerned about Robin's situation, and what looks like a trap.''

Fetterman expressed his blunt assessment of the situation. "We have no choice. We have to go in. The question is, how can we keep a close enough eye on Chuyen without him growing suspicious?''

"I suspect he's already suspicious, unless he's a goddamn fool. Otherwise he wouldn't have been so circumspect in these debriefings. He probably figures this is his last mission, his last big score, and then he'll return to the North. If he brings us in, he'll be set for life.''

"So we don't want to appear to be watching him too closely. We want to sit back and give him room.''

"Absolutely on the money, Tony. Krung has a good sense of intuition. Let's task him with watching Chuyen. In the meantime we'll politely listen to his counsel and give this traitor enough rope to rappel off a cliff and hang himself.''

"You sound as if you've already made your mind up about the man.''

"Maybe I have, and probably with good reason. He comes waltzing into Nha Trang with solid intel on where Robin is a week after she's taken out of circulation.'' Gerber wagged his index finger in front of Fetterman. "Uh-uh. Too convenient. I don't buy that man's story for one minute.''

"Maybe we shouldn't be the operational detachment deploying on this mission.''

"And why not, Tony? You figure we're too close to this one?"

"Exactly. Doctors aren't allowed to operate on members of their own family. Maybe we're too involved on a personal level. We wouldn't want to step on our own dicks because we got emotional. Maybe we should send another A-team into the Cambodian sanctuary."

"Cute. Real cute. Might I remind you that you're not a doctor and that Robin isn't a member of your immediate family. Assemble the team. We're going in ASAP."

Fetterman brightened. As much as spit and polish was part of being a soldier, he had discovered long ago that his forte was in the bush where he was able to pit himself against man and mother nature. For that was where he felt most challenged, most at home, most vibrantly alive. And soon he would be back doing the things he loved most.

4

Green Beret Staff Sergeant Dirty Shirt Crawley stood on the edge of the muddy riverbank where General George Washington had reputedly thrown a silver dollar clear across the broad waters of the Potomac. And even though Dirty Shirt didn't know the exact location where Washington had performed this legendary feat of skill, he figured he was close enough for government work.

In the palm of his big hand, Dirty Shirt held a Fifth Special Forces Group coin. The size and weight of the solid silver piece had to be approximately the same as the one Washington had used to perform his legendary feat of strength and skill. Dirty Shirt sighed, looked across the rippling brown water, pulled his arm back and hurled the small silver disk as hard as a major league pitcher. The coin arched high into the air, hit the apex of its trajectory about midway across, then plummeted like a man whose parachute had failed. The group coin plopped rather unceremoniously into the muddy water. "Sorry, Johnson, I tried my best," he murmured to himself as he walked to the waiting cab.

As Dirty Shirt squeezed into the back seat of the taxi, the driver smiled. "I seen lots of guys try that in the twenty years I been driving a hack. Ain't seen nobody yet been able to do it."

The cabbie pushed his snap-brim cap back on his head and maneuvered his vehicle back onto Ohio Drive. The driver wasn't finished talking yet. Gripping the steering wheel with one hand, he poked a finger in the air and went on.

"Even had a couple of professional wrestlers from Texas in my cab one time. Watched them oversize, oiled-up guys fume and fuss and sweat and swear up a blue streak while they pitched coin after coin into the drink. They musta went through about a hundred silver dollars. The silly sons of bitches didn't do as good as you did. And they didn't give me diddly for a tip, either. Ya know, sometimes you can see scuba divers out there. I wonder if they ever find anything down there other than car tires and Mafia tombstones."

Dirty Shirt nodded disinterestedly. He didn't appreciate gabby cabbies, and this one had been talking nonstop ever since they had left National Airport. But at least this one spoke English. Back in Saigon they either spoke Vietnamese or French. While it was true they sometimes owned up to speaking English, it was only when doing so would gain them some sort of financial advantage.

As the cabbie droned on about this or that political or Hollywood celebrity that had been in his cab, Dirty Shirt looked out of the open window and tried to ignore the driver and the crackling of the dispatch radio, one of the things he had been hoping to get away from.

In-country, with the backs of his hands and the side of his face bloodied by hordes of mosquitoes and smothered by the hot, humid jungle air, he had spent countless hours on radio watch; now he grimaced whenever he heard the crackling of static, the broken garble of anxious men on single sideband calling for arty or Medevac, and the relentless *dih–dah–dits* of CW transmissions. And now, twelve thousand miles away, his ears were still tortured by that awful sound of a crackling radio.

Feeling his nose tickle, the Green Beret pulled a white linen handkerchief out of his pocket, held it to his nose and let go with a big sneeze.

"It's all the pollen in the air," explained the cabbie. "It's cherry blossom time. Ain't it wonderful? Ya shoulda seen all the Sunday drivers yesterday, all the moms and pops and kiddies driving around gawking at the Japanese cherry trees blooming their little hearts out. Right pretty sight. Sure was. When I got home, my old lady says, 'Let's go for a drive, honey. I want to see the cherry trees.' I told her to go fuck herself, or call her sister if she wanted to go that bad. Jeez, I drive eight hours in a cab six days a week. The last thing I want to do is go for a drive."

Dirty Shirt nodded, noticing how the innumerable trees populating the tidal basin had sprouted white and pale pink flowers. Some of the petals had blown free and dotted the lawns like freshly fallen snow.

He found the powerful sweet scent to be a pleasant contrast to Vietnam's sharp odor of rotting vegetation and the putrid stink of dead bodies bloating in the sun.

Dirty Shirt took the handkerchief from his nose and absentmindedly looked at it. The linen was fresh, daisy-white but for a sprinkling of black grains matted on the woven cotton fibers. Momentarily it startled him. It seemed obvious the wind had kicked up some dust, black dust, and that had been what made him sneeze. He was used to that, but in Vietnam the dust was red. Yet another contrast between where he had been two days before and where he was in real time.

His reverie was broken as the cabbie swore in anger. An orange Volvo with a Save the Whales bumper sticker had swung in front of them, its turn signal going on only after it had already begun the lane change.

"Asshole," the cabbie muttered at the other driver. "Goddamn!" But another couple of blocks down the road the Volvo was forgotten and Dirty Shirt could see the cabbie studying him in the rearview mirror, sizing him up. "You're just back from Nam, aren't ya?"

Dirty Shirt nodded.

"Ya home for good?"

"No." He paused for a beat, anticipating the next question and knowing he'd have to answer it. "I'm escorting a friend's body home. Burying him in Arlington National Cemetery."

"Oh." The cabbie suddenly seemed to be at a loss for words. But the breather only lasted for a couple of minutes. "What's his name?"

"Johnson. Staff Sergeant William Johnson. It was his group coin that I threw in the river. He was always saying he wanted to try it someday. Thought I'd do it for him. Respect for the dead, you know."

The cabbie nodded as if he understood. "How did he die?" he asked in a reverent tone.

"Violently. Very fucking violently," said Dirty Shirt. How else does a guy die in a war zone? he reflected with some exasperation. Certainly not of old age or boredom.

The driver shook his head in disapproval. "Goddamn war. I fought in World War II with the Thirty-fifth Red Bull Division in Italy. Took six Kraut machine gun bullets in the chest." He tapped his chest repeatedly, each poke approximating the spot where an 8 mm bullet had burrowed into his body. "Got a permanent disability. I should be dead, so I ain't complaining. I was the only survivor in my platoon."

With that knowledge, Dirty Shirt's attitude toward his driver softened. So the guy was a combat vet. That made him okay in Shirt's estimation. He offered his hand over the back of the driver's seat. "My name's Crawley."

"Yeah, I saw your name tag. I'm Bob. Pleased to meet ya." With the cabbie still looking ahead at the traffic, the two men shook hands over the seat, united through the baptism of fire.

"War should be over soon," said the cabbie. "You read the papers?"

"No. Haven't had a chance to pick one up."

The cabbie took the newspaper off the front seat and tossed it back. "Good thing you're already sitting down," he said.

Shirt looked at the banner of the *Washington Post* declaring it an independent newspaper. Then he read the headlines and main story. His mouth gaped open. In a televised speech the day before, President Lyndon Baines Johnson had announced that he wouldn't run for reelection, that he would wind down the Vietnam War and devote the rest of his term to peace efforts. He had also called a halt to the bombing in the North.

Also on the front page he read how Martin Luther King was in town organizing a poor people's march. In his speech he had berated the U.S. government for spending fifty-three thousand dollars to kill each NVA soldier and only fifty-three a month to feed a hungry mouth.

A couple of pages farther inside, the paper reported the California Assembly had voted Governor Ronald Reagan their favorite son over Richard Nixon. Other than President Johnson's speech, the most interesting item was the news that a contingent of troopers from the Eighty-second Airborne had been returned to Fort Bragg because they had been sent to Vietnam with less than six months stateside duty since their last combat tour. Furthermore, eighty-five percent of the men in the Third Brigade had at least one tour in Vietnam.

Fucking pampered pansies, Dirty Shirt snickered. He was already on his fourth tour.

The cabdriver turned his vehicle into Fort Myer South Post and pulled up in front of Nebraska Hall, the transient barracks where Dirty Shirt would spend the night. The wooden World War II-style barracks looked old but well cared for with a fresh coat of paint on the exterior walls, but that was to be expected in the nation's capital.

From previous trips to Washington, D.C., he knew the area intimately. Stuck between Fort Myer North and South was Arlington National Cemetery, with the tomb of the Unknown Soldier. In the other direction, toward the Potomac River and Washington, D.C., proper, was the Pentagon, which he figured to be easily within mortar range.

He turned back to the cab and reached in through the driver's side window with the fare, including a modest tip.

"Thanks, Sergeant," said the cabbie, tipping his hat. "Get a good look at all this," he said, sweeping his hand across the panorama of South Post. "They're talking about knocking down all these old buildings, bulldozing more room for the cemetery. Running out of gravesites. Too many brave men giving up their lives for the cause, I guess."

How do you respond to something like that? wondered Shirt as he clumped up the steps to the barracks. Inside the building he found the CQ's station manned by a soldier dressed in freshly starched fatigues and spit-shined jump boots, which were propped on the desk.

Dirty Shirt immediately spotted a CIB and master blaster jump wings sewn above the soldier's left shirt pocket. The airborne wings qualified him as a paratrooper with enough experience to push a stick of jumpers; the combat infantryman's badge qualified him as a combat veteran. That rated the man as an equal in Dirty Shirt's eyes. On the other pocket he spotted Vietnamese jump wings, a decoration typically worn by SFers who had served in Vietnam.

The CQ looked up and brightened when he saw Dirty Shirt's green beret. As if he had just spotted an old friend, he jumped to his feet and held out a hand. The two Green Berets exchanged pleasantries, introducing themselves to each other. The CQ's name was Jim Callaway. The two soldiers told each other when they had gone through Camp Mackall and rattled off the names of men they might know in common with the A-teams deployed at Bad Tölz, Germany, Fort Gulick, Panama, or Okinawa.

The CQ noticed Dirty Shirt's deep tan and lean build, both the result of the tropical sun sweating the weight off a man. There was also the matter of the flash sewn on his beret that designated him a member of the Fifty Special Forces Group based at Nha Trang. "You DEROSed, out of the war for a while or what?"

Dirty Shirt gave a perfunctory shake of the head. "Nope. Need a bunk for a couple of nights. Escorting a friend's body. Going to go up to Arlington tomorrow for the burial."

Staff Sergeant Callaway's face darkened as Dirty Shirt handed him a copy of his mimeographed orders. He took them and laid them on the desk without bothering to read them. "Who is it?" he asked. His facial expression betrayed the fact he was clearly afraid it would be one of his friends. There simply weren't that many Green Berets in the world, and unlike the regular Army, everyone in SF knew nearly everyone else, if not personally, at least by reputation. That meant any SFer's death affected you.

"Johnson. Staff Sergeant William, no middle initial, Johnson."

"Don't know him," Callaway said with a quick shake of the head. Somehow he was more than a little relieved. "How'd he die?" he asked.

Dirty Shirt bit his lip. "Violently." Then his voice was quieter, almost a whisper. "Very fucking violently." He smiled and changed the topic. "None of my business, but what are you doing here? You some kind of liaison with the straight legs at the Pentagon? Why aren't you stationed with an SF unit?"

In response Callaway rattled off a Vietnamese phrase that indicated the rather dubious sexual preference of NVA soldiers for their mother-in-laws. Then he grinned proudly. "I'm studying Vietnamese. With the war building up, they can't handle all the warm bodies out in Monterey, so they set up a branch of the Defense Language Institute here. And I don't mind telling you I'm glad I got assigned in D.C. instead of out in fairyland like I did when I studied Czech. I just don't like that California mentality. You ever taste yogurt?"

Dirty Shirt nodded. Besides all of the cross-training, Special Forces required an SFer to be language-qualified. "I went to Monterey coupla years back. Learned German. Kinda picked up Vietnamese and Montagnard on my own."

As Callaway handed him an OD green blanket, two sheets and a pillowcase, he guffawed good-naturedly. "Oh, so you're a Monterey Mary, are ya? Yours is room 109, down the hall and to the left. It's away from the street, quiet and out of the way. Here's the key."

Dirty Shirt took the key, but his eyes were on the portable black-and-white TV sitting on the CQ's desk. The channel was flipped to an old Glenn Ford movie. "I like the old World War II flicks. This is the one where the bumbling general gets killed fighting Krauts, and his driver, Glenn Ford mistakenly picks up the general's helmet in the heat of the battle.

But the guy's a born leader and instinctively begins to direct the battle.''

Sergeant Callaway nodded. ''Yeah. I seen the flick at the movies when I was a kid. Used to pretend I was a soldier. Now look at me. Great movie title—*Imitation General*. The enlisted men see the star on Glenn Ford's helmet and listen to him like he was a great god of war or something. Ya see, they think he's the general and that because he is he ought to know something about fighting. Of course, after the battle the real general is awarded a righteous load of posthumous medals and the sergeant gets diddly squat. It's downright depressing. It's the one time the Hollywood Army looks too much like the real Army. By the way, it's redundant to say 'bumbling general.'''

Dirty Shirt rocked back on his heels. ''Me, I got better stuff to do my first day back in the World than to sit around watching a movie. How late you got duty?''

''Till 0800 hours tomorrow morning. I know what you're thinking. I wish I could go get a drink with you, but duty calls. All friggin' night long.''

Dirty Shirt stroked his stubbly chin, feeling the coarse texture of his five o'clock shadow. ''Anyplace nearby a fellow can get a drink? On base preferably. Quite frankly I don't want to mingle with any more civilians today. I've had my fill on planes and at the airport. While I would dearly love to vent my frustration, I don't want to end up in jail on assault charges.'' A moment later he added, ''Or worse.''

Callaway sighed. ''I know what you mean. When I came home from my last tour of duty with Fifth Group, I thought I'd be a national hero or something equivalent. Boy, was I wrong. Instead of inspiring their admiration, women and men were afraid of me. It's almost as if they think I'm a fucking heroin-crazed psycho who'll reach into their chest and yank out their still-beating heart and make 'em eat it.

Worst thing is, I met a very fine lady, great looker, great mind. She actually listened to what I had to say, until her father found out I was in SF and the narrow-minded bastard forbade her to see me. She doesn't listen anymore. Haven't seen her for three months. Another casualty of war.''

Dirty Shirt shook his head in disgust.

"Know what's worse?" Callaway went on.

"What?"

"Her old man was a Marine Corps gunnery sergeant in the South Pacific during World War II. Brags loud and long to anyone who'll listen about how many sons of Nippon he personally greased. Over at his house one night after dinner, he dragged out a bulging scrapbook. Laughing and joking, he points to a black-and-white snapshot of a Jap sniper who snuck into their company area after dark. You wouldn't believe what they did to his body after they held him down and blew his head off with a Thompson submachine gun. And he won't let her see me because he thinks we're all murdering baby-killing motherfuckers. Hypocritical bastard.''

"Consider the source," Dirty Shirt said. "He's a fucking jarhead. Maybe I should just go to a movie and go to bed early. Maybe I ought to turn in early and fight the jet lag that way.''

"Some other stuff you should know," said Callaway. "We've been getting reports about downtown, down by the bus station. Just for fun, civilians are ganging up on GIs in broad daylight. Goddamn peacenik motherfuckers.''

Dirty Shirt had difficulty perceiving such goings-on. "What, rolling them, beating them up? I can handle myself.''

He shook his head. "Nope. These are peaceniks hassling our guys. Nonviolent types. They don't hurt anybody. It's against their religion or something. Instead, they just embarrass the GIs to fucking death, yanking CIBs and campaign ribbons off their chests, then hauling ass as fast as their skinny little legs can carry them down K Street. They've even nailed a couple of on-duty MPs. So what are you supposed to do? Do you report to the police that you, a battle-hardened combat veteran, had your medals stolen by some fags? It ain't worth it. But it sure can be humiliating.''

Dirty Shirt absentmindedly touched his fingertips to his own CIB, his master blaster jump wings and four rows of ribbons. "Welcome home," he muttered to himself sarcastically. "Maybe I should go back to Vietnam early."

Callaway waved the notion away. "Don't sweat it. Just don't go into town. Up on North Post there's an NCO club, copious amounts of booze, fresh grilled steak sandwiches and about one thousand horny WACs to dance with."

Dirty Shirt gave a low whistle. "A thousand women on one base? You're exaggerating the numbers, right?"

Callaway shook his head. "If my ma told me once, she told me a hundred million times, never exaggerate. No sirree. They've got a ten-story barracks, hell, fifteen stories, I don't know. Anyway, they got a big building up there on the hill at North Post, big enough to house all the WACs who work at the Pentagon. And, brother, they're all man-starved females. Remember, they're competing with all the other secretaries who work for the government. Some guys say there's a ratio of ten women to every guy here in D.C. I believe it. Fort Myer is the best duty station I ever pulled. But outside the main gate I treat D.C. like a hostile nation. A man need go no farther than the confines of this base to get his rip cord yanked."

"We'll see," said Dirty Shirt as he headed for his room.

5

AN UNWANTED VILLAGE
CAMBODIA

The first thing the glowering North Vietnamese interrogator told Morrow and Maxwell was that it was important to tell the truth and only the truth. He was short, standing five feet, weighing about 120 pounds, and garbed in a khaki uniform with a blue-trimmed collar. He scowled at them, always maintaining his ramrod bearing that bespoke a sense of self-importance.

Strutting back and forth in front of them, he barked, "Why did you come here? Why did you sneak into Cambodia?" His accent pinpointed him as a South Vietnamese member of the North Vietnamese army.

For the seventh time Morrow recounted her story, patiently detailing how she was on assignment to interview Norwood, the American soldier who had deserted. Morrow had decided she'd answer time after time as many times as it took. She wasn't intimidated because she recognized his method, even if he was clumsy with it.

Make the prisoner repeat his story over and over, then look for holes in it. And when you find one, open it wide. But she knew there would be no holes in her story. With the NVA's army of spies located in Saigon, and probably within the ARVN command itself, it was just a matter of time before her story checked out. Until then all that was required of her was to endure whatever came her way.

The interrogator scowled at her telling of the facts. Suddenly his voice was subdued. "Then why did you arrive in a CIA helicopter? We know it was Central Intelligence, even though it was without insignia. Everyone knows black helicopters are used for clandestine activities. What is your connection to the CIA?"

Morrow shrugged. "It was a ride, that's all. We have no connection at all to the U.S. government, other than the fact they were our only means of transportation unless we wanted to drive for hours in a car. And you know how unsafe that is with rebels and trigger-happy troops on both sides."

She paused for a while to let the notion sink in. Morrow had decided her interrogator was a rank amateur. She had plenty to base her assessment on, having previously been captured by opposition forces a number of times. She had already endured torture. And rape. Judged by the standards of his predecessors, this guy was a fumbled-fingered lightweight.

One-Eye, one of the Vietcong soldiers who had captured her and Maxwell, came in grinning. He and the interrogator went off in a corner and chatted animatedly for about ten minutes. When the interrogator strutted back to talk with Morrow, his demeanor had shifted from bad guy to good. He was smiling.

"You must forgive my earlier behavior. I had to be sure you were who you said you were. And I am afraid I am not very effective at this sort of thing. You see, I am not an intelligence officer but a psychological warfare officer. And your capture presents an extraordinary situation. Listen to me. I would like to make you a proposal."

Now it all fit. She knew why he had been bumbling. It wasn't his line of work. Furthermore, given his position, he probably wanted her to be a reporter; it would better serve his purposes if she were a reporter than if she really were a spy.

"Okay," she said, "I'll bite. What's the deal?"

"The two of you will remain prisoners of the Army of the Liberation and you will accompany Captain Dinh's unit for one month. His men are the ones who captured you. During that time you will observe the war from our point of view. At the end of that time you will be freed. Obviously, since we cannot control your actions after that, whatever you write shall be up to you."

Morrow decided to play along. "What are my options? What if I don't want to go along with this Captain Dinh of yours? What if I demand to be released right now?"

She wasn't entirely sure she did want to be released. In fact, if she went along with them, she'd have one hell of a story. And Maxwell would have a great deal of intelligence dropped into his lap. Most likely he'd be able to observe firsthand the enemy's tactics, walk along their supply routes and take cover at their stopping points. Even if they modified their activities, the experience would be invaluable.

The interrogator called One-Eye over. "Huan will be in charge of you. You will follow his instructions. And if you try to escape before we are ready to release you, he has orders to shoot."

ROBIN MORROW FOUND HERSELF deep in the triple canopy of the Cambodian jungle, stepping over a tangle of bushes, pushing away branches from her face. She knew they were on the Ho Chi Minh Trail the moment she looked overhead and saw how the treetops had been pulled together and tied. From the ground the lashed trees created the effect of walking through a living green tunnel. From the air, a pilot, even one with keen eyesight, would see nothing but jungle foliage. An army and all of its equipment could pass below unseen.

And so they walked from Cambodia, east toward Vietnam. Each of the NVA troops dressed in the same khaki fatigues, carrying three wooden-handled grenades on their pistol belts and three chest bandoliers filled with ammunition for the AK-47s. Across their backs were slung canvas tubes holding several pounds of sweet dried rice.

Morrow noted the NVA unit was organized in six-man squads, separated by intervals of about fifty feet. She was the third person in her squad, walking directly behind a soldier who was carrying a mortar base plate. The weight didn't seem to bother him as he ambled along the deeply rutted trail, seemingly oblivious to the load that would have made a Westerner stagger, gasp, wheeze and whine.

Stepping over a tree trunk that had fallen across the trail, Morrow figured the cadre stretched out their units to minimize their losses in case they were ambushed. Ambushed. She found herself imagining an American infantry unit opening up on Dinh and his men, and grinned, then shuddered with the sudden realization that she would be in the middle of the firefight.

They walked until midmorning when Dinh called a halt. Morrow brushed away leaves and twigs, clearing a bare spot on the ground. Squatting over the exposed earth, she examined her forearms where thorns and razor-sharp leaves had slashed her flesh, leaving jagged blood-red lines etched across her wrists and the backs of her hands. On her face she could feel where a branch, carelessly let loose by the man in front of her, had whipped back, tearing at her skin and nearly putting out her right eye. Maybe that was what had happened to One-Eye, she surmised.

She estimated the NVA unit, all totaled, to be company strength, or about 150 men. By the dialect, she could tell that most of the men were from the North, but with a sprinkling from the South. She figured this would be the place where they rested for the night. Already fires had been lit.

The company commander, Captain Dinh, strutted over to squat next to her. "Hello, miss, how are you?"

He spoke good English with a slight French accent, which she attributed to his having probably learned the language during the French occupation of Indochina.

"I trust that you are relatively comfortable," he said to her. He had the habit of looking directly into her eyes whenever they spoke. The practice unnerved her because she wasn't sure whether he was trying to be romantic, or intimidating. Either way it had the effect of making her skin crawl.

"Yes, I'm fine," she told him.

After the conversation with Morrow, he had a short word with his executive officer, the two of them speaking Vietnamese. "We'll halt the men for a while," he told her finally.

"Training exercise?" she asked.

Dinh nodded. By now his executive officer had ordered the soldiers to bunch up together, then he directed them to each pick up a rock.

The captain pushed through the mob, stepped in front of his men and pointed to the tallest tree at the edge of the clearing. In Vietnamese he directed, "When I count to three, throw your rock."

Obediently 150 men drew back their arms in anticipation of letting fly. On his command they would have just as easily attacked an American armored personnel carrier with nothing more than a sharpened bamboo stick.

The captain counted off, and on the count of three the enlisted men hurled their rocks as hard as they could. The sky seemed to grow dark under the fusillade of projectiles as if every rock in the world was streaking through the air toward the tree. Rocks struck the limbs, clattering loudly as they tore bark away from the trunk.

The enlisted men's eyes grew wide with amazement at the spectacle they had just witnessed, that they had created.

Dinh smiled and said in his singsong voice, "Now you have seen the dramatic effects of what your rifles can do. Each rock represents a single bullet from each of your AK-47s. Imagine what it would have been like to be hiding in the tree with all of those projectiles coming at you. And now imagine what it would be like to be an American soldier with this company shooting at you. Now multiply the effect on him when you each fire more than one bullet." Dinh's face was stretched wide by a diabolical grin as he looked at Maxwell and continued talking to his men. "Now you can understand why American soldiers are so afraid."

After the show of rocks, the men settled down to eat. One-Eye came over with a big smile and handed both Morrow and Maxwell a box of U.S. government issue C-rations. "Dinh says you eat."

Across the clearing they could see the captain sitting on his haunches under the protection of a cavelike hollow shielded by a bushy tree. He nodded and smiled at the two of them with great pleasure.

C-rations were obviously not the usual meal served on the Ho Chi Minh Trail, Morrow figured. It was more of a political statement than a logistical consideration. After all, there seemed to be plenty of sweet rice stuffed in the salami-shaped cloth tubes that the NVA had draped around their shoulders, and it was doubtful they were being fed ham and lima beans because they were VIPs deserving of such preferential treatment.

No, Morrow reasoned Dinh was feeding them C-rations merely to show them that he could. This then was a lesson in guerrilla warfare. Dinh was demonstrating how easy it was to kill American or AVRN troopers and take their ammunition and food supplies away from them in order to sustain his own war effort.

6

CAMP A-555 FIFTH
SPECIAL FORCES
COMPOUND REPUBLIC
OF SOUTH VIETNAM

Green Beret Staff Sergeant Eugene T. Troutman was the AST assigned to assist Captain Gerber's A-team. That meant whenever Gerber or Fetterman said they needed maps, intelligence data or aerial photos from the intel shed, it was the AST's job to provide it. And when they requisitioned webgear, rucksacks and ordnance, it was also his job to provide it.

Once in isolation and in the planning phase of a mission, he was an A-team's only contact with the outside world. No one else was allowed in or out. The concept was intended to prevent leaks concerning an A-team's destination and purpose, leaks that could compromise the mission and get everyone killed.

Troutman liked what he did for a living. His was a cushy job, and as far as the sergeant figured, it went beyond merely being a choice assignment. He had long ago figured out that as long as he functioned as an AST he would never himself be required to wear a rucksack and never have to trudge off into the jungle, desert or arctic and get shot at or blown into little pieces.

So, for the past five years, wherever he had been assigned, be it Bad Tölz, Germany, Fort Gulick, Panama, or even Fort Bragg, Troutman made sure he was assigned to HQ as an AST. As a lifer ready to give up on the Army, he was counting the days until his ETS when he could go back to Clinton, Iowa, and throw his uniform into the corner and spend the rest of his days fishing for bass in the Mississippi River. And when the river iced over in the winter, he'd just sit in front of the fire and get fat on poached venison and pheasant.

Troutman wondered how many members of the A-team he was currently working with would ever make it back to the States. Many of the spike teams that infiltrated behind enemy lines simply disappeared from the face of the earth. Troutman knew some of the guys on this team—Gerber, the team commander, who was standing in the middle of the room with the two Chinese guys, and Fetterman, the team sergeant, who was using green tape to fasten his Ka-bar upside down on his webgear suspender. The others he knew by sight, but nothing more. And like so many of the A-teams lately, this one would deploy short of men.

Troutman watched as the team's junior commo man lashed his radio set and kit bag to the outside of his rucksack with suspension line. The AST had talked with the good-looking kid the night before, after briefback, when he said his name was Walsh, that he was from Kansas and had worked during the summers at Yellowstone. When he'd been drafted, he had joined Special Forces rather than get stuck in the infantry.

Troutman had decided early on that he liked the kid and wanted to do whatever he could to help him survive the mission. He also knew that whenever possible the enemy diligently tried to knock off radio operators. Without communications with its HQ, a unit was cut off from reinforcements and could be crushed like a snake. Troutman put down his coffee and went over to the RTO.

"Mind if I give you a tip?" he asked in a humble voice.

"Sure. I'm no dummy. I figure the more I learn the better chance I have to live long enough to get promoted."

Troutman showed him how to camouflage his AN/PRC-74 radio by shoving it deep inside his rucksack and bending the antenna down alongside the rucksack's frame where it offered a lower profile. That way the VC would have a harder time knowing who was humping the radio.

"I should have known that," said Walsh. "Probably learned it in Training Group. It's just that they threw so much at us in such a short time...."

"I know what you mean, kid. And it's the little things that fuck you up. Like the man said, the only way you get killed in Vietnam is if you make a mistake. Don't make one and you get to go home alive." Troutman clucked his tongue. "Wish I could go along with you guys on this one and show you the ropes, but I'm stuck here as AST. I guess my job's important, too."

The two of them reacted to the sound of angry voices. Chuyen had just been introduced to Krung, and Troutman could plainly see the two men had taken an instant dislike to each other. He wondered if there was going to be a fight. Gerber could handle it if it did happen, he figured.

Like Chuyen, Krung was a Vietnamese Chinese, a Nung. One of the differences between the two was that Gerber and Fetterman trusted Krung implicitly. More than once Krung had proven his loyalty under fire—during the siege of Camp A-555 and on direct-action missions behind the lines in Laos, Cambodia and North Vietnam.

Another difference between the two was that Krung passionately hated Communists or anyone with leftist tendencies. Fetterman once joked that if Krung had his way even people who were left-handed would be summarily castrated. Given Krung's history, it was understandable. Krung had been fighting the Communists with heartfelt passion since before his sixteenth birthday.

In the beginning, when the Communists displaced his tribe from their ancestral home in the North, the Nungs chose to become refugees, moving to the South in order to avoid bloodshed. If any man had a reason to hate, it was Krung. His father had been headman in the village.

One night Krung had gone to the next village to borrow an oxen, and because of the rain had chosen to sleep there. Sometime after midnight the VC bullied their way into his father's home, rounded up and barbarously murdered every member of his family. It wasn't a pretty sight. The sole exception to the massacre was his youngest sister. It would have been easier if she too had been executed, because the ordeal that followed was unconscionable. A squad of VC brutally gang-raped her, then left her bleeding body and stunned mind as a living memento of what would happen to those who supported the Saigon government. Four weeks after her night of living terror, Krung's twelve-year-old sister committed suicide in a particularly horrible manner.

Immediately following the funeral, Krung swore a blood oath on the souls of his dead ancestors, vowing to kill fifty enemy soldiers for every dead family member. Death wasn't the end of suffering for the VC that fell to his smoking gun. Krung castrated them with his knife, then nailed their genitals on a four-by-four sheet of quarter-inch plywood. By last count he had avenged himself tenfold.

Now, facing Chuyen, who towered over the shorter man, Krung unsheathed his razor-sharp knife and held it menacingly in his grip. Eyes blazing in anger, he told Chuyen, "Americans trust you. Listen what you say. I not like you. Never turn back on you."

Chuyen laughed derisively and placed his hand on top of Krung's head in the classic bullying gesture.

The smaller, quicker Krung reacted instantly, sweeping the arm away with one hand and with the other swept his knife toward Chuyen's chin with a deft sideways cutting movement.

"You missed," chuckled Chuyen, protectively holding his hand against the side of his neck.

"Try shaking your head."

By then Fetterman and Walsh had separated them. Troutman waddled up to Gerber. "You're going to have your hands full with those two on the same team."

Gerber looked him dead in the eye. "Yeah, *we* are, aren't *we*?"

Troutman guffawed. "Reminds me of the joke where Tonto and the Lone Ranger were out of ammunition and surrounded by a thousand hostile Indian warriors, and the masked man says, 'Looks like we're about to die, Tonto,' who replies, 'What do you mean *we*, white man?'"

Gerber put his hands on his hips. "We're shorthanded, Sergeant Troutman. We need a man with your capabilities. Besides, you're not one of those guys who likes to wear the green beret but never wants to wear the rucksack, are you?"

Troutman harrumphed. "Well, I, ah. I mean..." Suddenly he was conscious of the fact that his heart was beating faster and his palms were clammy.

Gerber shook his head. "Too late. The orders have already come down from Colonel Rheaulter. You're going with us. And I sincerely hope you can keep up with us. You've kept in shape all these years, haven't you?"

''You're as cracked as a porcelain piss pot if you think I'm going to—''

Gerber interrupted him. ''I'm what, Sergeant?''

Troutman apologized for the lapse of military protocol, then went on to plead his case. ''What about my responsibilities here at C&C? Someone has to be the AST. Assisting the teams in their deployment is every bit as important and critical as the actual mission.''

''Granted. And don't think I'm thrilled about your company. Deadweight is worse than being shorthanded. I trust you'll do. And if I were you, I'd be cranking my mind-set up to where it will do the most good. Otherwise you may have a problem with reality.'' Gerber checked his watch. ''In about six hours be ready mentally and physically.'' Finished, Gerber went over to talk to Fetterman.

Troutman, watching the two of them talking, muttered to himself, ''Eugene, you just skated out of your last detail.''

7

Dirty Shirt instructed the cabbie to let him out at a dimly lit corner somewhere in the middle of Georgetown and then paid him off with a meager tip. Walking toward the Buttercup Lounge, the Green Beret sergeant noticed the sidewalks were littered with candy bar wrappers and cigarette butts. Empty wine bottles peered out of twisted brown paper bags. Against a lamppost a trash can had overflowed, spilling dozens of empty pop cans out onto the concrete.

Passing a doorway, he spotted an unconscious old woman; an empty beer bottle lay smashed a couple of inches from her dangling hand. Her skirt was hiked up around her waist, exposing a pair of filthy panties.

Once inside, the Buttercup Lounge was nothing fancy; it looked like a cross between a high school gym and a USO dance hall. Shirt searched the crowd, trying to get a feel for the clientele. He spotted the off-duty GIs right away by their scuffed Army-issue shoes and the way their pants didn't fit right. He knew why. After eight weeks of basic training, the average GI was in good shape with a trim waist and muscular legs while the typical civilian had a pudgy waist and skinny legs. Accordingly, off-the-rack trousers were tailored to fit the overfed, underexercised civilian frame. The best fit a GI could hope for was a pair of pants that fit snugly in the thighs and hung loose around the waist.

The closely shorn hair was another solid clue, mused Shirt. While long sideburns were in vogue in the World, GIs were mandated to keep theirs clipped above a line even with the ear canal. With all of those elements distinguishing a GI from the rest of humanity, he stood out hopelessly in a crowd. That was, of course, unless he wore a wig like some of the vain draft-dodging National Guardsmen.

Dirty Shirt padded up to the bar and ordered a glass of vodka from the kid pretending to be a bartender. From his looks Shirt was pretty sure the guy was a soldier moonlighting for a few extra bucks.

The bartender clumsily handed him a shot glass, spilling some of the clear liquid over the rim.

Dirty Shirt stared at the bartender. Intimidated, the kid's eyes grew wide, and he started to visibly tremble. "You said a glass of vodka," he said, taking one step back. "Did I do something wrong?"

"That's right. A glass of vodka," said Dirty Shirt. He pushed the glass back across the bar. "Where I come from a glass of vodka stands five fingers tall. Gimme."

"Oh." The bartender fixed the drink, and Dirty Shirt wandered off into the crowd.

Fans of live music and alcohol had packed into the Buttercup, determined to have a good time. Frosted mugs of beer slid down the slick bar, quenching the horde's thirst. Everyone was partying, with several drinks lined up in front of them.

In one corner Dirty Shirt noticed a group of men in suits. He immediately pegged them as businessmen tired of trysts with their easy, doe-eyed secretaries. The foursome had obviously crowded in for a look at the pretty coeds in skintight blue jeans and gingham blouses. One peek at the braless breasts would make their day.

Flabby, spa-muscled guys like the businessmen disgusted Shirt. Eavesdropping, he listened to the conversation that centered on the impressive showing they had made in the Korean War while stationed at Fort Dix, New Jersey, or how their son was a hotshot on the Boston Bruins hockey team. They behaved like unschooled fat boys when the barmaid served the drinks. "You're an angel, sweetheart," said a fat one as he pushed his horn-rimmed glasses up the bridge of his nose. "You brought me my beer and I love you for it," he slurred drunkenly.

Dirty Shirt shook his head in disgust. Old fools. He hoped he would never be like them, men who anxiously gulped down handfuls of bitter-tasting vitamin E capsules with their orange juice, played golf in the afternoons and in between worried themselves sick about measuring up as men. But then how could they? The most strenuous exercise they did was shuffle a deskful of paper and shout "Yes, sir" to the man.

Dirty Shirt could never work for the man, never become a potbellied ball of lard like these clowns. He shook his head in disgust and vowed that if he ever turned into a pencil-pushing lardass, he'd end it.

Dirty Shirt sipped his vodka and listened to the dull bass thumpings of the live music. For a bunch of college boys they weren't too bad. They were all characters. One member of the long-haired group looked out of place with his army-style crew cut, but he seemed to be the only one with any real talent, playing two saxophones at once. Behind him the forgotten drummer beat out the tempo. Rivulets of sweat trickled down his bare chest as the Quaaludes worked their magic behind his forehead.

The lead singer wore a skintight black jumpsuit; his bulging genitals stretched the fabric, leaving nothing to the imagination of the girls who danced at the foot of the stage. And although these ladies were with their boyfriends, their roving eyes were on the man in black.

Clustered around a ringside table, one of the band's groupie girlfriends shamelessly slugged free drinks. She wanted her money's worth. She wore a floppy black hat to better emphasize her role in life as a consummate bitch. For one reason or another she had decided to be mad at her boyfriend singer, the one in the black jumpsuit. To get even with him for his real or imagined sins, she would ignore him, maybe even try to pick up some guy. That would really fry his mind.

Dirty Shirt saw the woman in the floppy hat with makeup pancaked on her cheeks. Their eyes made contact. She flashed a big smile.

Dirty Shirt looked away. His intuition told him she was a merciless tease—big talk, no action. What the hell? He glanced back in her direction.

Her cold, calculating smile was right there to meet him.

Dirty Shirt looked away and gazed into his drink, studying the vague patterns in the melting ice cubes. Forget it, he told himself, chuckling. She gave off a bad aura. He knew better. Forget her. Ask some other woman to dance. He began to stroll the dance arena, looking for a target of opportunity. It didn't take long to find one.

She was a thin and feisty-looking redhead, holding her head high as if she knew a secret about herself. Dirty Shirt decided this was the kind of woman who would only look good in gold jewelry. Silver was too common. Her clothes would be from specialty shops with Givenchy and Yves Saint

Laurent labels. She would draw men easily. Walking the streets, men would whistle at her and wish she were theirs for the night, the sort of woman who could overpower a mere male with her presence, smother his manhood with her femininity. She would be so much woman most men wouldn't know how to handle her. Yet Dirty Shirt felt he could.

He had to wait before he could make his move. Five paces away from her table, a thin black dude with gold-capped teeth and a diamond-studded earring stepped between them and asked her to dance. The black looked very flashy in his emerald-green suit, but the woman turned him down with a polite reply: "Thanks, but no thanks."

Surging with confidence, Dirty Shirt closed the distance between them and asked her to dance. "No, thank you," she said demurely. "I don't feel like dancing right now."

"Well, then," said Dirty Shirt, improvising, "will you buy me a drink?"

She never missed a beat; most women would have been flustered. "Buy you a drink," she said, chuckling. "That's a new one." She laughed heartily, throwing her curly, tousled locks back.

Dirty Shirt was beginning to experience a sense of anticipation as he sat down at her table and drew his chair close to hers. It would be easier to talk that way. He noticed that her lipstick, nail polish and high-heeled shoes matched—a brilliant red. She was also dressed in a white blouse, her milelong legs accentuated by her denim miniskirt. She exuded warmth. Some women are like that. Ahead of time a man can sense how she will be in bed—warm, energetic and lifegiving. The kind of woman that gives to a man instead of taking. One such encounter would be enough to last through the dry spells.

"Tell me all about yourself, why don't ya?" she drawled. Dirty Shirt pegged her accent as originating in South Carolina, maybe Georgia.

He shrugged. "Naw. I find that kind of talk about how many brothers and sisters in the family and what my dad does to be rather boring. I'd rather talk about my friends, if you don't mind."

She did a double take. "Isn't that precious. You just passed the first test," she drawled. "You're not stuck on yourself like so many other guys are. My, oh, my, maybe I've found a true gentleman at last."

Eyebrows furrowed in mock consternation, Dirty Shirt asked her, "Test? Who said anything about me taking a test? And what do I get if I pass?"

"Think about it," she said, batting her eyelashes.

He didn't see any delicate way to respond.

She went on. "So tell me, you home from the war for good? Don't be upset, but I can tell you're in the military from your buzzie."

"My what?"

"Your buzzie. Your haircut, silly." Playfully she ran her hand over the top of his head. "So, like I asked, you home from the war?"

He sighed. He was growing tired of answering that question. "Nope. Six months to go on my tour of duty. I escorted a body back to Arlington. I'm only back here in the World for about a week. Then it's back to the war, excuse me, the police action."

"Oh," she said, taken aback. "I never would have guessed you were escorting a body. He a friend of yours?"

He nodded. "Good friend. Knew him since I was a kid. Went through Camp Mackall together. I watched him die."

From her facial expression and the tone of her voice, she seemed concerned enough. "How did he die, if I may be so bold as to ask?"

"Violently. He died violently." He was growing weary of answering that question, as well.

She put her hand on his arm. The sexual purring in her voice was gone, replaced by what sounded like real concern.

"How? How did he die? Tell me."

"I'd rather not talk about it," he said flatly.

"Oh," she said. After an awkward silence, she told him, "I'm sorry about your friend. I really am. I just can't imagine what it would be like to be in the middle of combat." She paused for a moment. "If you want to talk about your friends, go ahead. It's all right with me. I mean, the ones who are still alive."

Dirty Shirt dispelled the black mood that had fallen over them when she had brought up Johnson's death. He took her crisp smile and dedicated interest as a signal that she was out for a good time and whatever developed between the two of them was fine.

"Word is Fetterman's been in the Army since Christ was a private," he said. "Of course he flatly refuses to divulge his correct age to anybody. It's in his 201 file, but he takes great pains to make sure the facts are kept secret. No matter how old he is, I can't think of anybody I'd rather have by my side in combat."

"What's combat like? I mean, what's it really like?" she asked.

He answered matter-of-factly. "You think every bullet has your number on it. You feel like yanking buttons off your shirt so you can get down lower. The noise is worse, though, the fucking noise."

"The bullets and explosions," she said. She sounded as if she understood it well enough to have experienced it herself.

Dirty Shirt shook his head. "Nope. The screams of the dying. Men reduced to whimpering, wounded animals by excruciating pain. Men who see their arms blown off and know they're gone forever. Men who know they're bleeding to death and who know they're not going to make it." His mood had darkened once more. "Welcome to Vietnam," he said sarcastically. "Welcome to Vietnam, courtesy of the Killed In Action Travel Bureau."

"Maybe we should change the subject," she suggested.

Dirty Shirt wrapped both hands protectively around his highball glass and stared at the ice cubes as if they could reveal important answers. His voice was solemn.

"Some people think war is all shooting and commando raids. Fact of the matter is it's mostly boring and very unpleasant. Most of the time jungle warfare is a tough, dirty life. Never enough sleep, sores, dirt caking your pores, digging holes, crawling on the ground, swearing, wading across rivers, making your way through terrain no man in his right mind would ever go near. The only way to keep from going insane is to dream about warm beds, clean sheets and steak the size of your arm."

"Oh, shit," she mumbled. She forced a smile and directed her gaze toward the door.

Shirt was embarrassed; he knew he had a case of verbal incontinence. "Well, enough about me," he said, slapping his hands on the tabletop. "Let's talk about you for a while." He grinned for her benefit.

Now her eyes were really sparkling. She took his hand into hers. "Oh, there's nothing much to tell. I work in Langley for the CIA." She rolled her eyes. "Talk about boring work. Listen, I have an idea. Let's go to my place. The music isn't so loud. If it gets too late, you can sleep on the couch or something. Do you like plants? I've got so many my place looks like a greenhouse."

Shirt imagined what her apartment would look like. He figured there'd be oil paintings and sketches dotting the wall, and a forest of monstrous green plants hanging in macrame-encased pots. He could already feel her warm breasts gliding against his bare chest, her lips glistening, ready for his rain of kisses.

The reverie was cruelly interrupted by the arrival of a crew-cut kid wearing white socks, spit-shined shoes, an OD T-shirt and blue jeans loose in the waist and tight in the thighs.

"Christ," muttered Dirty Shirt under his breath. He looked up and hoped the woman wasn't the kid's wife or girlfriend.

But the newcomer's voice sounded too amused, too good-natured to be angry. He ignored Dirty Shirt and spoke directly to the woman.

"Well, if it isn't Pam in the red fuck-me shoes. Hello, Pam."

"Hello, Buzzie," she replied, making fun of his haircut.

Buzzie ignored the dig. "By now she's had time to ask you to tell you all about yourself. She's told you how she's a secretary downtown, either in the State Department or in Langley with the CIA. Bullshit. In case you didn't know, and I figure you're bright enough to have spotted her outright and that's why you're sitting with her, this here is a five-dollar whore, a little less if you're running short until payday. And you don't have to even spring for a cab to one of the motels down the street. She'll just lead you by the hand into the shadows outside. Isn't that right, Pam? Love your new red shoes. Did you buy them or shoplift them?"

Dirty Shirt looked toward the floor in time to see her tuck her feet under the chair.

The crew-cut kid wasn't through. He guffawed, pointed at Pam and looked directly at Dirty Shirt. "This old broad's seen more dicks than a barracks urinal. Why don't you just hit the bricks, Queenie?'' he told her. His voice meant business.

Fuming, she stood up and viciously gave the kid the finger and a murderous look. Myth dispelled by a solid dose of reality, Pam seemed to age before Dirty Shirt's eyes. Now he could see how the makeup pancaked on her cheeks didn't quite cover the pockmarks, and the nail polish on her stubby fingered hands seemed out of place. She stomped out, looking very unladylike, clumping her way across the dance floor in her red shoes.

Dirty Shirt lied to save face. ''I knew she was a whore,'' he told the kid, ''and you knew I knew she was a whore. What made you figure I needed rescuing? What are you, an Army chaplain, or a fag who thinks I'm cute or something? You better be a chaplain.''

Crew Cut shrugged. ''Hey, I like pussy as much as the next guy. Fact of the matter is Pam's given more guys a case of the clap than any ten pavement princesses. I was just doing you a favor. GIs got to stick together these days.''

Dirty Shirt scratched his chin in mock concern. ''No shit. I never woulda guessed a guy could catch something from a whore. You ever hear of condoms, sonny? Even with one of those goddamn things stretched over my dick, belly-whomping a whore is better than being reduced to having to make the scene with the magazine.''

He had hurt the kid's feelings. ''Well, fuck you, then. I was only looking out for your best interests. Still catch her if you hurry.''

Fuming, the young man turned to walk away, but Dirty Shirt grabbed him by the seat of the pants and swung him around. ''Sit down.''

With a quizzical expression, the youth plopped down in the chair recently vacated by the prostitute.

By now Dirty Shirt had mellowed. "Ya meant well, kid, and that's what counts. That's what counts, goddamn it. Let me buy you a drink."

There was still a slight edge to the kid's anger. "Yeah, I meant well. Like I said, she's seen more dicks than a barracks urinal."

"Know what you mean," said Dirty Shirt, giving him an appreciative wink. "A guy would think she was a virgin till she sat on a fire hydrant and sank clear to the ground."

They spent the next hour talking about duty in the Military District of Columbia versus duty in South Vietnam. The kid had served one tour of duty with the Eighty-second Airborne Division in Vietnam, had reenlisted and was now a sergeant assigned to the Home Guard, the unit responsible for burials in Arlington National Cemetery. They were drawing from ten to twenty burial parties a day. But after all, there was a war on and that was to be expected.

Finally they got around to the subject of Sergeant William Johnson. Dirty Shirt sat rigidly in his chair, fingers wrapped tightly around his drink, holding it so tightly the kid was afraid he would crack the glass. Staring intently into the melting ice, Dirty Shirt said in a monotone, "Willy was a good friend. I'm sorry the son of a bitch is dead."

After a moment of silence, Dirty Shirt looked up. From the expression on Crew Cut's face he could tell that the kid wanted to say something but either didn't have the nerve or simply didn't know how to say it diplomatically. "Spit it out, kid. You're among friends. Friend, anyway," he corrected himself.

"How'd he die?"

Dirty Shirt didn't answer for a while, but when he began to talk it was like a floodgate opening. "It was just a matter of time. Coupla months ago a Chicom hand grenade landed in the middle of the mortar pit. Willy jumped on it, trying to save the rest of us. Damn thing never went off. A dud. He looked silly as hell five minutes later, just lying there on top of it. After a while we made him get up and brush himself off. Couple weeks later the same thing happened again. Another Chicom grenade, and he jumped on it like it was in his job description or something. Another dud. As you can imagine, we teased him mercilessly.'' Dirty Shirt took a long pull on his drink, draining it. ''They say three's a charm,'' he slurred. ''Three's a charm. Third time it was an American grenade. Not a dud. We make reliable munitions in the U.S. Like I said, he died very fucking violently.''

Crew Cut didn't say a word. The very thought of being torn into little pieces by expanding gas and red-hot shrapnel sent shivers up and down his spine. He considered his own body to be sacred, and even the thought of a scar made him squeamish, let alone losing a hand or leg. But to have your guts vaporized by an explosion was an unfathomable horror.

Yet Johnson had thrown his own body on a grenade, probably not even for a fraction of a second thinking about what was going to happen before feeling the white-hot pain from the sharp edge of the shrapnel tearing him limb from limb. ''I'm working tomorrow,'' the kid said. ''I'll see if I can't draw duty on his burial party.''

Dirty Shirt stared at the kid for a moment, then said, ''You know what, kid? You're a good shit, too.''

8

IN THE JUNGLE NEAR
ELEPHANT EAR
CAMBODIA

No one shot at them and no one ran away from them. Instead of NVA soldiers taking potshots and booby traps blowing off arms, legs and testicles, nothing happened. If Captain Gerber had called the helicopters to ferry in hot pizza and cold Budweisers, the patrol could have spread their poncho liners on the ground and enjoyed an afternoon picnic. Regardless of the pastoral setting, the Green Beret captain kept up his guard. "All constants are variable," he muttered.

Trudging into a clearing at the head of the A-team, Fetterman brushed his fingers against the sleeve of his tiger-stripe camouflaged jungle fatigue shirt where a pocket of gray-green mold had started to grow. The fabric was beginning to rot from too many days spent in the greenhouse humidity.

With a heavy sigh he resigned himself to the fact that they would have to have new fatigues airdropped before these rotted clear off their bodies. Then he looked at his boots. The green nylon uppers looked brand-new, as well they should at only a month old. But the soles were a different story. Humping mile after mile on rock-studded trails had eroded the tread so badly that they, too, would have to be replaced. Fetterman decided he was thirsty. "Anybody got any water?"

"Yeah," said Sergeant Kimber T. Walsh, the junior commo man, immediately unslinging a two-quart canteen and handing it to his teammate.

Fetterman gave the canteen a little shake, gauging the quantity of water left. There wasn't much. Slowly he unscrewed the cap and took a sip. His eyes crossed as his tastebuds rebelled at the flavor of water purification tablets. But he still swallowed the fluid, nearly choking on it. He wiped the back of his hand across his mouth and said wryly, "Tastes so bad you need something to wash it down with."

After spending the day on a trail climbing steep mountains and sliding down slippery slopes into valleys, sweating, resting and drinking their canteens as dry as a bone, Gerber had called a halt. Now, huddled next to Fetterman, he tapped the map, indicating a swirl of green ridgelines commingled with a blue curl that cut through the dead center of it. "If my calculations are correct, we're here and there should be a stream at the foot of this hill. There's no use all of us going for drinking water." He smiled knowingly at Fetterman. "We'll wait here for you."

It was Fetterman's turn to climb down the mountain and fill the team's canteens, which he did without incident until he was knee-deep in the clear, swift-moving stream. Then the hairs on the back of his neck bristled.

He heard voices filtering up from downstream. Instead of the hushed tones of enemy soldiers wary of betraying their position, these voices were both loud and boisterous and rang with laughter. Whoever it was, they were behaving as if there was no war within a thousand miles of them. The Green Beret sergeant wondered if the quality of NVA soldier had slipped that much.

Fetterman crept closer to the sound of the voices, pushing branches away from his face, slowly taking one step at a time through the thick foliage. Then he could see a fire—and two mahogany-skinned men with wiry builds that showed more bone than muscle. "Montagnards," he murmured. Stone Age tribesmen who still used crossbows to fight their battles. Huddled around the fire with the men were two younger boys, whom the master sergeant figured to be around fourteen years old. Fetterman assumed the boys were the men's sons.

Unaware of the American's presence, they showed their teeth with big smiles, chatted among themselves and took turns rotating what looked to be a very large chicken spitted and hung over the fire. Fetterman watched in silence as the flames licked the skin and hot fat dripped into the crackling fire and flared up.

One of the Montagnards howled in laughter at what was obviously one of his own jokes while he carefully held his elbows high, away from the flames, as he brushed red sauce on the browning meat. The other man grinned politely, then put an unmarked black bottle to his lips, tipped his head back and swallowed twice. When he took the bottle away from his mouth, his eyes were wide open. He coughed before handing the bottle to his son.

Fetterman looked on with some amazement at the scene. Then it dawned on him that the group was having a picnic. His stomach started to grumble; a gallon of saliva gathered in his mouth. I'm not hungry, he told himself.

Suddenly, and for no apparent reason, the men and their sons stood perfectly still, like deer in the middle of the highway mesmerized by headlights. No one moved or made a sound. Then the oldest of the men smiled and looked directly at the patch of foliage where Fetterman was hiding. With a big smile the Montagnard gestured for him to come out. "American, come eat. We have plenty. We share. You like. Come. We not Cong."

With the element of surprise gone, and feeling as competent at the art of personal camouflage as a buck-ass private in basic training, Fetterman pushed his way through the brush and stepped out into the clearing.

He smiled, figuring his war face wouldn't cut it. Nonetheless, he remained alert, M-16 held alongside his body, finger close to the trigger just in case the Montagnard's smile faded and an AK-47 suddenly appeared with the muzzle pointed in his direction. "You speak English, eh?" said Fetterman. It was both a question and a statement of fact.

The Montagnard nodded and continued grinning. "Speak real good English. Learn from Quaker lady when I was young boy." He pointed at Fetterman's black-stocked M-16. "I believe in peace, not war. You not need weapon here." He giggled as he reached over the fire and signaled the other adult male to help him lift off the spit. "Besides, dog already dead."

So it was dog meat and not chicken as he had thought it was. Fetterman had eaten black mamba in Africa, monkey in the Philippines and alligator in the Florida Everglades, but never dog. There was a first time for everything, he supposed.

For a moment the Montagnards ignored Fetterman while the two men teamed up to slice the dog into individual pieces. While the American watched, their hands deftly worked the blades, and he decided that he was glad he wasn't on the receiving end of the razor-sharp tools.

Meanwhile the two boys busied themselves with a wicker basket, pulling out an assemblage of bowls and chopsticks primitively carved out of wood.

One of the boys and his father conferred in their native tongue. The young boy pointed at Fetterman, his expression betraying concern over some issue. Fetterman instantly appraised the situation: they had only brought enough bowls for themselves. Since they hadn't planned on a guest, he was number five and odd man out. No big deal. He would tell them he could eat with his fingers. A bowl was unnecessary, a luxury item, as far as he was concerned.

The old man cuffed the youngster's ear good-naturedly. "No worry," said the man, looking at Fetterman and waving his finger in a carefree manner. "You get bowl. My son and me share. You guest."

Once the logistics of carving up the dog and dividing food and bowls had been figured out, the group of five sat on the ground. The conversation lapsed for a few moments as the males hungrily placed large morsels into their mouths.

Fetterman decided not to embarrass himself by attempting to use the chopsticks and instead used his fingers. He knew this would perhaps brand him a barbarian in their eyes, but he figured that was better than appearing to be an all-thumbs incompetent.

When one of the boys noticed Fetterman's approach to finger food and started to giggle, his father frowned at him, but didn't say a word. The boy's face froze. He sat there immobile as if he were afraid to say or do anything. Then the father winked at his son, and the sparkle came back into his young eyes and he started to eat again.

Fetterman went on with his meal, struggling not to wolf down the food, knowing that if they sensed how hungry he was they might give up more of the food in spite of the fact that their families probably lived on the equivalent of thirty dollars a year. So he made each bite count, trying to determine the flavor of the fire-blackened skin. He decided the taste was a cross between hot peppers and diesel fuel. Still, he found it to be a real delicacy, the meat oozing juices into his mouth.

The barefooted men squatted in a wide-legged stance, absentmindedly wiggling their splayed toes. Like any people who didn't wear shoes, their feet were extraordinarily wide, giving the impression that a bigger man's feet had been hacked off and sewn monster style onto their ankles.

Surprisingly the soles were only slightly callused, and he could see where stones had nicked the skin in some places and bruised it in others. Fetterman noticed how they were able to wiggle their feet sideways, an accomplishment civilized man was incapable of. He knew the Stone Age Montagnards were able to do that because their feet were never constricted by shoes and therefore had never lost their flexibility. Just thinking about it made his own boots feel very uncomfortable.

Fetterman had seen these primitive men's counterparts in the jungles of Panama and on Africa's burning plains. They weren't part of the economic system that required a man to keep running with the pack, earning money and consuming goods or services at a furious rate. Instead, the picnickers and their sons lived life leisurely, lounging around their village until desire for food or sex moved them to act. Their needs were simple, their lives uncomplicated. And sometimes Fetterman wondered whether they weren't in fact, more civilized than Western man.

Between bites the Montagnards talked among themselves, the conversation punctuated by peals of laughter. As they gabbed away, they inadvertently left Fetterman out of the conversation. He understood but couldn't speak their language, and his inability to communicate made him feel like an outsider. That realization triggered the memory of something he had been taught as a boy: if you want to feel at home, make your hosts feel at home.

During a lull in the conversation, he said in English, "This is very good." He took a big bite of dog meat, closed his eyes and exaggerated his facial expression. "Better flavor than the food we get back in the World, I mean, back in the States."

The old man translated for the others, and then the four of them nodded and beamed, jabbering among themselves. One of the men sent a young boy over with the bottle. "Drink. You like. Taste better than Ba Muoi Ba beer." He spit on the ground. "Have bigger kick, too. Drink."

Fetterman laughed uproariously. "Even warm tiger piss tastes better than Thirty-three beer." He raised the bottle to his lips and drank deeply, knowing full well what was to come. The burning began at the base of his tongue, scorching the length of his throat. Finally it imploded in the pit of his stomach, where it felt like a lump of molten lava trying to burn its way outside to his navel. But he never allowed his facial expression to show even a flicker of discomfort. Likewise, he didn't try to avoid their eyes, for they would be watching him to see how he handled the alcohol.

Then, with as much expression as if he were pulling down a drink from a Coke bottle, he took three more gulps of the stuff, all the while wondering if the stuff had burned clear through his belly.

Fetterman nodded, smiled and told them, "Thanks. Really good stuff. Hits the spot."

The two Montagnard men got up. Chattering gaily, they came over to Fetterman and patted his back. "You okay guy. You real tough," the one who could speak English said.

"Palm tree wine, huh?" he asked them. He knew the men had made it by lopping off the top branches of a palm tree and letting the sap ferment in the trunk. Days later they would have hammered a hole in the base of the tree and caught the 110-octane fluid as it dripped out.

The old man nodded. "Palm tree, yes. Very good." He drank deeply from the bottle, then he wiped his hand across his mouth.

By now the Montagnard's hunger was nearly satisfied, and they slowed the pace, chewing more times per bite and starting to talk among themselves between mouthfuls. When they were finished eating, the two adult males put down their empty bowls, stood up and stretched.

The boys gathered up the wooden bowls and waded into the stream. Standing in ankle-deep water, they scoured the bowls clean with handfuls of black sand. They were so intent on their task that they resembled California miners panning for gold dust. Finished scrubbing, they rinsed the dishes in murky water and came ashore.

The one who spoke English shook the palm wine bottle, proving to himself that it was indeed empty and that not a single drop would be wasted. Satisfied it was dry, they began to play a game where the American and the Montagnards each took turns trying to balance the bottle on the end of a stick. One of the boys was best at it, seemingly able to balance it and walk around the clearing forever.

Finally when they were bored with that, the oldest male took the bottle in hand, wound up like a baseball pitcher and hurled the bottle as hard as he could. The five of them watched as it arced high into the branches before slamming against the side of a tree trunk with a resounding thunk, then fell to the ground, kicking up a cloud of dust as it hit.

One of the boys reached into the wicker basket and passed out bottles of Coca-Cola. He gave one to the American. Even though the liquid had been warmed close to the boiling point by the midday sun, the sweet drink felt good going down Fetterman's throat.

Coke bottle drained, he handed his empty to the boy who had given it to him in the first place. Just then the older man grabbed Fetterman's right arm. Fetterman had never seen anyone move that fast. Startled by the action, he nearly drew back. But looking into the Montagnard's black eyes, he could tell that he was in no danger.

"Wear this," said the Montagnard as he slipped a bronze bracelet on Fetterman's wrist. The bracelet's surface was covered with cryptic markings.

Fetterman thanked them for the food and drink, waved goodbye and started his trek back up the side of the mountain, feeling the weight of the filled canteens pulling on his shoulder. He wondered what he should tell the other members of the team. Would they be jealous that he had been fed real food while they had to suffer through C-rations? And while there had been just enough for Fetterman and the Montagnards, should he have declined the offer of food because there wasn't enough to bring back to the other members of the A-team? Fetterman decided to play it by ear when he got back to the camp.

By the time he arrived at the clearing, some of the men had taken off their jungle fatigues and had strung them up in the trees so that the sun's ultraviolet rays would kill any bacteria or mold that had taken root in the pores of their skin or in the sweat-dampened seams of the clothing. Also, most of the team had already eaten their simple meal of C-rations.

Fetterman walked around the clearing, handing out the topped-off canteens and offering the sage warning, "I put in the water purification tablets already. Let the water sit at least an hour, so it can kill all the nice little buggies floating around inside. That is, unless you enjoy curling up in a little ball and screaming in gut-wrenching agony."

The master sergeant spotted Gerber just outside the fire ring. The captain was squatted Montagnard-style, with his heels spread shoulder-length and his butt nearly brushing the ground. Fetterman joined him as the Green Beret captain poked a stick at a can he was retrieving from the fire. "Saved some pound cake for you, Tony. Must be warm enough by now."

The fire-blackened can lay at his feet, a thin wisp of smoke rising above it. Heat had charred the OD paint to the point where black flakes curled up in patches on the side of the can. Gerber jammed his hand into his baggy pants pocket and pulled out a flat tin of peanut butter and gave that to Fetterman, too.

Under normal circumstances, merely thinking about warm pound cake frosted with peanut butter made Fetterman's mouth water. But with his belly warmed by barbecued dog meat and palm wine, canned pound cake seemed as appetizing as a big glop of wet flour.

The taste of the barbecue sauce was still thick in his mouth; he pressed his tongue against the back of his teeth and could feel tiny bits of meat lodged between them. Unconsciously he let out his belt as if he had just stepped away from a Thanksgiving meal. "Pound cake," he murmured without enthusiasm. "Nothing better this side of prime rib."

Gerber smiled. "Thought since you went for the water, I'd cook for you."

Fetterman nodded as he patted his pocket, searching for his can opener. He found it and peeled back the peanut butter lid. He used the plastic spoon that was included in the box with the rest of the meal to mix up the clear peanut oil that had separated from the gray-brown paste. Finally he smeared the oily glop on the pound cake and took a bite.

The warm cake sucked his mouth dry of saliva like a sponge. The sticky peanut butter clung to the roof of his mouth like a thick lump of clay. He chewed slowly, then swallowed with difficulty.

Gerber looked on in wonderment. "You okay?" he asked with some concern.

"Fine. Why? What makes you think there's anything wrong?" Fetterman hoped the tone of his voice didn't betray his defensive mood swing.

Eyebrows furrowed, Gerber pointed at the pound cake inside the OD C-ration can, crumbs dangling on the rim. "Used to be the way to a master sergeant's heart was through his stomach via that delectable goody. You ill, or simply off the pound cake kick?"

Fetterman shrugged and continued to stare into the fire.

Gerber knew he was onto something, so he didn't let up. "Trade you my fruit cocktail for your wienies and beans."

Fetterman handed him the wieners and beans. "Here, you can have them. I'm not that hungry for some reason." Then he reached into his rucksack and took out another box of C-rations and held it up for all to see. "Anyone want my ham and lima beans?"

In a low voice, so nobody else could hear, Gerber asked, "What's wrong, Tony? Something happen out there when you went for water? What did you see?"

Fetterman was silent for a moment, not wanting to lie to his friend and yet not wanting to tell him the truth, either. He felt a stirring of guilt welling up out of nowhere, the price he paid for having shared in the roasted dog and home-brewed booze. Finally he said, "Trust me on this one, Captain? Don't ask questions. Someday back at the Continental Shelf I'll tell you all about it over drinks. You'll either be pissed or think it's funny."

Gerber studied his sergeant's face for a moment, then nodded. "Sure. 'Till later."

They moved out an hour later, walking until they came to a village that wasn't on the map. At first glance the settlement appeared clean. The huts were set among palm, mahogany and teak trees, with flowers sprouting in clumps everywhere.

Fetterman decided it was the kind of place travel writers would have described as a tropical paradise, if it had not been in Vietnam. Fetterman's only complaint was the weather, the stifling heat and humidity. He wiped a gallon of sweat off his face with his sleeve and told Gerber, "Well, why don't we choose sides? We haven't killed anybody all day. I'm getting kind of bored. Besides, if we shoot off some of this ammo we're carrying, we'll lighten our load and we can make better time."

Gerber grimaced. "The day is young and Charlie is out there waiting and watching, just biding his time. Even though I can't smell his foul breath, I can feel his presence. Let's search the village."

They split into groups of four or five and worked each house, quietly and smoothly. They found nothing. The village was deserted and appeared to have been for some months, so they moved on.

Just past the last house, the point man said he thought he had heard something moving in the undergrowth. The rest of the team took cover as Fetterman crawled forward to investigate. Fifty feet out he found foliage cut down to knee level. He could smell fresh dirt.

A stone-cold silence settled as he crept nearer the zone of death. Now Fetterman could also feel the enemy presence. Even though he couldn't see their khaki uniforms and AKs, he could feel their warm bodies from twenty yards away as much as if they had laid a cold hand on his heart.

He lay still for five minutes, listening for the enemy and watching as a long-legged spider crawled on a branch about three inches away from the tip of his nose. The big arachnid seemed curious about what the soldier was doing so near its domain. Fetterman picked up a twig and began to poke the spider's fat, hairy body. It backed off an inch, reared up on its hind legs and spewed out a stream of white venom. The master sergeant wondered whether the toxin needed to be injected or was poisonous on contact.

He decided to let the spider live, then crawled forward to investigate further. After a few yards, he crouched over a freshly dug hole. Suddenly, and as if Gerber's words about Charlie in the bush had been prophetic, an AK opened up behind Fetterman, followed by a few frantic bursts of M-16 fire.

In those few moments before the firefight began, Sergeant Kimber T. Walsh had seen something move in the brush about thirty feet away. His jaw froze, and he felt like vomiting. So this was how it will be? he thought. This will be my first firefight. A moment later a man appeared, and Walsh could clearly see that he was a North Vietnamese regular. Only one, he hoped. The enemy soldier stepped out into the open, looked from side to side, then seemed to spot Walsh, dropped to the ground and started firing.

Without warning a flurry of shots echoed from down the trail. So it was settled. There was more than one VC. Then someone fired a burst from an M-16. Probably Fetterman, Walsh reasoned.

The other NVA fanned out, knowing exactly what to do without specific orders, trying to see if the Americans were an isolated squad or company strength. Once they had the numbers figured out, Walsh knew they would try to envelop them.

Walsh raised himself. A fraction of a second later an AK-47 chattered, the rounds passing just overhead, the crack of the bullets breaking the sound barrier and hurting his eardrums.

Gerber smacked his face down to the ground. Too close for comfort. He took another look. This time an AK directly in front of him opened fire. A third weapon opened up on his left. Walsh shot at the enemy in front of him. He figured out what they were up to. As one man fired, the other two crawled closer. He could hear their movements in the brush. Another VC fired and the other crawled. By now Walsh couldn't rise to shoot back.

He heard a scream to his left. "I'm hit!" There was a strange urgency in the voice.

Walsh turned to look and saw an American soldier standing. He was Troutman, the AST who had helped Walsh with the radio and who was filling in for Dirty Shirt while he escorted Johnson to Arlington. Hit in the chest, the new guy had reacted instinctively by standing. His eyes held an oddly intent look. He thrust out a hand as though to steady himself on a support that wasn't there. He opened his mouth in an attempt to suck in a deep breath. Bright blood gushed over his lips, trickling down over his chin and onto his chest. An AK fired a long burst, the fusillade tearing off the top of the soldier's head. The rim of his helmet dropped down around his neck, and he toppled to the ground.

By now Walsh's VC were only about fifteen feet away. He could hear them creeping closer and closer to his position but couldn't do anything about it. Suddenly he heard himself screaming, "Somebody get me the hell out of here."

Fetterman came rushing out of a clump of shoulder-high grass and surprised the enemy, killing two of the three with one long burst. Walsh seized the opportunity and stood up to kill the third man with a single shot to the heart.

"These guys must be pissed off or something," muttered Fetterman.

The two of them watched as more NVA soldiers poured through the trees. Fetterman fired and Walsh picked his way back down the trail the way they had come. Walsh provided covering fire and Fetterman caught up to him.

"Is this what's called a strategic withdrawal?" asked Walsh as he crouched next to Fetterman.

"Very fucking funny, *Private*." Over the din of battle they heard Gerber shout the order, and they started to retreat in pairs.

Fetterman stayed behind and covered them. For twenty minutes the enemy played with him, taking potshots and hurling verbal abuse. An enemy soldier lay dead at Fetterman's feet. The corpse had the appearance of a puppet that had been carelessly dropped by its master—eyes wide, mouth gaping and a black-rimmed hole in the chest that you could stick your thumb through.

Fetterman tried to watch everything all at once. He felt a bullet tug hungrily at his sleeve, and at the same time saw a puff of smoke in the distant trees. Too close for comfort, he thought. Splinters leaped from the trunk, scratching the side of his face as another slug smacked into the tree next to him.

An AK cracked, and Fetterman felt a stinging sensation on the inside of his forearm just above the left wrist. At the same moment something red-looking smacked into the tree next to him and hung there. Instinctively he grabbed his wrist, and his hand came away bloodied. He looked at the tree trunk, and saw a piece of human flesh stuck to the bark. He had just been wounded. "Mother fuckers!"

An NVA officer rose out of the palm fronds and dried leaves in front of him, squeezing off shots and advancing toward Fetterman. The master sergeant squeezed the trigger, unleashing a three-shot burst before the weapon jammed.

"Enough," he mumbled, dropping the useless weapon. He pulled the pins on two hand grenades and still grasping the arming levers, ran forward in a half crouch. He stepped on the chest of the still-quivering NVA officer he had shot moments before.

Uncharacteristically Fetterman went into a blind rage, hurling grenades at the enemy positions like he was stoning a snake. Twenty paces into the brush, he collided with an NVA soldier and knocked him flat on his back. Fetterman kicked him as hard as he could in the jaw, then kept on running deeper and deeper into the heart of the jungle.

9

ARLINGTON NATIONAL
CEMETERY
WASHINGTON, D.C.

After parting company with the crew-cut kid at the Buttercup Lounge, Dirty Shirt Crawley took a short cab ride back to South Post. At the last minute, though, he decided to go for a walk instead of heading for his bunk. The outside air was cool, a full moon illuminated Washington, and the sky was splattered with twinkling stars.

A starlight scope would be at its best on a night like this, Dirty Shirt reflected as he started walking toward Nebraska Hall. He cackled when he noticed he was avoiding empty pop cans and other debris lying in the street, quickly realizing that his seemingly obsessive behavior was nothing more than a holdover from having served in a combat zone.

In Vietnam you never stepped on anything, never kicked anything out of the way; it could be booby-trapped and blow your foot off. Unless the trigger had been rigged to an undetonated Air Force five-hundred pound bomb, in which case there would be a very loud bang, a puff of smoke and no more GI.

Dirty Shirt figured booby traps were probably not much of a danger in the World, so he drop-kicked a pop can out of the street and onto a general's well-manicured lawn. Then he was miffed because the thoughtless act had probably scuffed the spit-shined toe of his boot.

A moment later he decided against walking the road that connected the two because that was the way he had come. This was an ancient rule of warfare: never return from a patrol the same way you left the camp. Besides, he had some business to attend to in the very heart of the graveyard. He jumped the fence and began to walk through Arlington National Cemetery. The grass felt soft and springy underfoot, and the moisture from it cooled the air and chilled his face.

Out of reverence for the dead, and exaggerated by the drinks under his belt, he felt a strange compulsion to march. Softly he murmured the cadence, Left, left, your left, right, left. He could almost hear the muted tones of a bugle playing taps. This was, after all, a place thick with military history. Fort Myer and Arlington had once been General Robert E. Lee's farm until the Civil War when the Union Army had confiscated it from the Confederate general. And ever since it had been the final resting place for dead American soldiers.

Dirty Shirt felt at peace, noting that it was easy to march across the terrain without elephant grass to slice his uniform to ribbons, without jungle-clad mountains to climb, or a tangle of vines or fallen trees across the trail. Walking down the hill, he came to a gentle valley hidden from the starlight by a cluster of trees. A little farther and he was out in the open again, bathed by moonlight, walking as if he knew exactly where he was in the graveyard and exactly where he was going.

Finally he paused at one of the gravestones, sunk to his knees and traced his finger against the inscription: Corporal Charles B. Crawley, Omaha Beach 1944. Dirty Shirt got to his feet, came to attention and reverently saluted the grave. Without a trace of an alcohol-induced slur in his voice he stared directly at the headstone and said in a somber voice, "You're deader than hell, Dad, but you're not forgotten. Not forgotten for a minute." Then he swept his hand in a gesture that included the circle of graves around his father's. "You guys, too. We know you're here, know what you did. Paid the price. You sure as hell aren't forgotten, either."

He talked, telling his father what was new in his life and how the war was going. After a while Dirty Shirt ran out of words. He felt sheepish and wondered whether the fallen soldiers could even hear his words, and if they could, whether they gave a good goddamn about what he said. Maybe once your life was snuffed out patriotism didn't matter to a man anymore. In any case, he wasn't even sure he believed in ghosts or the spirit world, but felt that it was important to at least remember the dead and to try to keep their spirit alive and walking the face of the earth. He hoped when he was dead and gone someone would do the same for him.

Weary from the long day, Dirty Shirt sat down on his father's grave and rested his back against the cool stone. From his back pocket he took out a harmonica, brought the instrument to his lips and began to play. While he made music he thought about how his dad had been with the Devil's Brigade, the Airborne Ranger unit that had preceded Special Forces. And how, when he was a kid, he had vowed to carry on his dad's tradition, how his father's life and death had been the inspiration for his volunteering for airborne school and the Green Berets.

Suddenly he took the harmonica away from his lips. He had been recalling his earlier conversation in Nebraska Hall when the CQ had told him about the street punks who were brazenly ripping off medals. Protectively Dirty Shirt held the palm of his hand against his jump wings.

"Not to worry, Dad. When Mom gave me your jump wings, I vowed I'd never lose them. Another thing, Dad. I'm dropping off a buddy tomorrow morning. His name's William Johnson. I've told you about him before. Introduce him around and show him the ropes. He's the kind of guy who'd do to go on patrol with."

WITH DAWN LIGHT PEEKING through the window, Dirty Shirt Crawley woke up thinking about the businessmen he had seen the night before in the Buttercup. Pencil-pushing lardasses with nicotine-stained lungs, who couldn't run a mile if a VC was chasing 'em with a fixed bayonet. Dirty Shirt rolled out of bed and checked the time on his watch—0600 hours. He yawned and stretched, then slipped into gym trunks, a Special Forces T-shirt and jungle boots and dragged his ass outside.

Still not fully awake, and with legs as stiff as artificial limbs, he jogged down the company street, out the gate and then on to the Arlington Memorial Bridge. The sweet scent of the cherry blossoms was thick, mixing with the moist morning air and pleasantly masking the odor of automobile exhaust and the stink of a million people living in close proximity to one another.

Dirty Shirt was pleased. In all the time he had spent on his tours in Vietnam, he hadn't been able to work out properly and as a result had been worried he'd be out of shape. But he had no problem now breathing or running and figured that was due to his regimen of chasing Charlie up and down the mountain trails of the Central Highlands.

At that hour it was still dark and the Lincoln Memorial was lit up like a church on Sunday. Dirty Shirt walked up the brightly illuminated stone steps and soon stood at the feet of the colossal sculpture of Lincoln seated in his emperor's chair. Dirty Shirt considered his own presence at the monument: under the circumstances it was somewhat ironic. Abraham Lincoln had served as President of the United States during a civil war that had split the North and South and divided brother against brother.

A hundred years later the scenario was repeating itself in a somewhat modified fashion. The U.S. was involved in Vietnam's civil war, and again the U.S. citizenry was divided, brother against brother, sister against brother, hawks against doves. Again the U.S. was being torn apart. Dirty Shirt stared at Lincoln's sculpted face, the somber expression, the powerful eyes and scraggly beard.

After a while he walked down the steps, across the sidewalk and off to a little knoll of trees at the northwest corner of the reflecting pool. Squatting on his haunches, he gazed across the waters of the reflecting pool toward the Washington Monument. It, too, was lit up, and plainly visible was the spot where construction had been stopped for some years—he couldn't remember the reason why—and when they had resumed the stone was shaded a slightly different color, permanently marking the break.

Feeling something rubbing against the side of his foot, Dirty Shirt looked down to see a baby rabbit nudging him with its pink nose. Sweeping his fingers through the grass, he located a divot that had been dislodged by whoever had driven one of the big riding mowers over the grounds the day before.

Nearby he found the hole in the ground that the creature's mother had used as her nest. He knew that he dare not touch the furry little thing, or his human scent would be imparted to its hide, and when its mother showed up, she would never suckle the bunny and it would surely die. Instead, Shirt got to his feet and tenderly nudged the animal with the toe of his boot, slowly and deliberately forcing it back into its nest. Once the bunny had settled down into the damp brown earth, he partially covered it with the divot and hoped the mother rabbit would come home soon to nurture her baby.

A shiver ran up and down his spine. His insides felt ice-cold. He threw his head back and roared with laughter. ''The heebie-jeebies,'' he said aloud, recalling how his mother had told him and his brothers how such a sensation meant you had stepped on the spot where your grave would be. If he had felt the tingling while walking through Arlington, he might have given such a preposterous idea some credence. But given the current climate toward the GIs in general and the Vietnam conflict in particular, it seemed unlikely any Vietnam veteran's grave monument would be erected within a stone's throw of the Lincoln Memorial.

Shirt glanced at his watch and decided that it was time to jog back to the barracks and have a shower. Johnson's funeral was only a few hours away.

WARREN BILLY SMITH WAS royally pissed off. At the last minute his editor had delegated him to rush to Arlington National Cemetery and cover the burial of Staff Sergeant William Johnson. Who the hell was this guy Johnson and why did it even matter? These days they were planting KIAs faster than they could send them over to Nam.

Smith was fuming. The burial of a mere fucking sergeant, and probably a nobody at that—who the hell was he to rate newspaper coverage? Smith wondered if the guy had won a chestful of medals before he croaked, or maybe he was a posthumous Congressional Medal of Honor recipient.

After a moment's contemplation, he ruled that out in favor of something more obvious: Johnson was probably the son of a congressman or a brigadier general. While he pondered the possibilities, Smith stood outside the chapel at Arlington National Cemetery, chain-smoking Camels while the Army pukes did their thing inside among the multidenominational icons, church pews and stained glass.

After a simple service at the chapel, Smith watched as all the brightly plumed Army guys followed the flag-draped coffin out the door and onto the street. Moments later they loaded up in two OD-painted Ford sedans, one sedan each for the carrying party and the burial party, and followed the black Cadillac hearse.

The procession carefully wended its way through the paved streets of Arlington. Smith followed in his own car, slowly driving past the fields of dead where two thousand unknown soldiers of the Civil War and the more than 250 blown up on the battleship *Maine* were buried.

When the hearse got to the burial site, the drivers pulled over to one side of the road. In silence the six pallbearers carried the coffin from the street and laid Johnson over his grave. Standing at attention and staring at the American flag, Dirty Shirt thought it all appropriate. In the old days flags were often used as temporary shrouds to protect the dead in combat zones until a coffin could be constructed or the body buried in a simple grave.

The NCOIC barked a command. Then, unexpectedly, the stern-faced men performed a drill ceremony that included the Queen Anne's salute followed by more fancy rifle swinging. At that precise moment Dirty Shirt noticed that all of the men in the firing party and the burial party were senior noncommissioned officers. The lowest-ranking soldier was an E-5, and there was only one of him—the crew-cut kid he had drunk with at the bar the night before. All the others were E-7s and E-8s.

Dirty Shirt knew the drill ceremony was unusual, as was the predominance of NCOs when such details were usually relegated to first-term E-4s and E-5s. He looked in the direction of Crew Cut and caught the man's surreptitious glance, which made everything clear. Somehow the buck sergeant had arranged a deluxe ceremony.

Out of the blue, Dirty Shirt found himself somewhat irritated by the sound of helicopters. Perhaps he heard it sooner than the others because his jungle ears were more in tune with the sound of a machine that his life depended on. To him the sound meant Medevac, resupply, extraction or gunships chewing up the enemy that minutes before had been threatening to annihilate his unit.

As the *whap-whap* of the blades grew louder, the ceremony came to a dead stop and everyone turned toward the Potomac to look up. Six Army Hueys were flying toward them in a tight formation. Suddenly one of the aircraft pulled out of the formation. The other Hueys maintained their course, ignoring the errant helicopter. Then it dawned on Dirty Shirt that this was the rotary-wing version of the missing-man formation.

Reporter Warren Billy Smith was heard to comment in a hushed, confused tone, "What the fuck...?" He didn't understand everything that he was seeing.

Dirty Shirt looked at Sergeant Crew Cut, who responded by looking at the formation of Hueys, at the honor guard that had done the fancy rifle swinging, at the flag-draped coffin and then back at Dirty Shirt. Johnson had been killed in combat saving his friends. And now men who didn't even know him were paying him special tribute.

Dirty Shirt knew what came next. The buglers would play taps to wish the servicemen good sleep until the eventual reveille to come. Solemn-faced, seven Army band members raised bugles to their lips and began to play the first few musical notes. By the numbers, and with military precision, the firing party raised their glossy M-14s to their shoulders and pointed the muzzles skyward. On command they fired three volleys, a twenty-one-gun salute.

Dirty Shirt's ears detected a subtle difference in the rifles' reports. Instead of a bang, there was a crack, which meant they weren't firing blank ammunition as they should have been. Instead, they were firing live ammo.

With the haunting three-note refrain echoing along the Potomac River valley, Dirty Shirt murmured the lyrics:

Fades the light.
And afar goeth day.
Cometh night and a star leadeth all.
Speedeth all to their rest.

The sound of the helicopters faded off in the distance as the band members swung their shiny bugles down to their sides. On command the firing party lowered their rifles and snapped into parade rest. The silence was deafening.

Majestically the pallbearers delicately took up corners of the American flag, raised it from the coffin and began to fold it into a triangular shape. Finished, the sergeant-in-charge handed it to Dirty Shirt, who tucked it under his arm.

Crew Cut gave Dirty Shirt an almost imperceptible wink. No irreverence intended. Looking into the kid's eyes, Shirt could see the kid was pleased with himself that he had pulled off a special ceremony for Johnson. Dirty Shirt only hoped the guys flying the helicopters wouldn't get into trouble.

Shirt took a step closer to his dead comrade and placed his big hand on the lid of the coffin. He sank to his knees, sighed, then began to speak in a gentle voice, unashamed that everyone would hear what he had to say.

''Well, Willy, I reckon I'll be getting back to see you. By the way, my old man's up the hill from here. Look him up.

I told him all about you. You two look out for each other, ya hear?''

Dirty Shirt got to his feet, straightened his beret and walked toward the sedan. He decided he wouldn't ride back in the hearse. He was going to cram in with Sergeant Crew Cut and his pals.

And then a short, pudgy civilian with gray hair stepped in front of him. ''Just a second there, soldier. I'm a reporter for one of the local papers. I noticed you had some special kind of connection to the deceased. Wonder if you'd mind my asking you a couple of questions...?''

''Sure. Go ahead.''

''Who was this guy?''

Dirty Shirt let out an irritated sigh. He already knew what the questions were going to be, so using his fingers, he enumerated the answers one at a time. ''Sergeant William Johnson. I escorted his body back from Vietnam. He died fucking horribly. Hand grenade. He jumped on a hand grenade, so I wouldn't have to. And as soon as I can get on a plane, I'm going back to Vietnam and kill some more fucking Communist pinko bastards. No, I don't like Barry Sadler or his song about the Green Berets, and it's not my job to figure out the politics in a war, only to fight in it.'' Finished, Dirty Shirt left the reporter and strode away swiftly.

Smith just stared after him for a while before he responded with, ''Okay. Works for me.'' Then he waddled off toward his own car, muttering, ''High-strung son of a bitch.''

10

NOH LY CAMBODIA

In the middle of the night One-Eye roughly shook Morrow awake. Rubbing the sleep from her eyes, she heard him say Dinh had ordered her to come with him. "Captain Dinh say truck go off cliff. Many people riding in back, try get away from American bombs. Truck go off cliff. Those who live need help. You are Americans. You come. You know doctor medicine. You help."

She understood the part about how there had been a B-52 strike, but Morrow didn't entirely understand Dinh's logic. Nonetheless it seemed that she and Maxwell were being called on for two reasons. First, because of their nationality they were deemed responsible for the suffering, and secondly because they were Americans, they were expected to know something about medicine and first aid. The first part of this rationale made sense, but the second didn't. No matter. She decided she would go along and do whatever she could to treat the wounded.

One-Eye led her through the dark village to one of the huts dimly lit by kerosene lamps. The injured had been dragged inside. Two young women, three or four children and one old man lay on the dirt floor. Wracked with pain, the women sobbed, the children bawled outright, while the old man just moaned.

One of the NVA soldiers thrust a medical bag into Morrow's hands. She squatted next to one of the injured women and looked at the wounds. One-Eye stood next to her shining an electric battle lantern wherever she directed the beam. On close examination the woman looked as if a tiger had torn into her with its claws. One deep gash ran along the side of her chest, exposing three ribs. Her right ear had been ground down to the cartilage. Four front teeth had been broken off flush with the gums. Her face and hands were covered with blood. She had the look of a woman who was afraid she would no longer be pretty.

Trembling, Morrow unzipped the first-aid kit and searched for antibiotic ointment. When she found a tube, she squeezed a thin bead into the wounds. Next she used the suture kit to stitch them closed. She was thankful for the time she had spent in the Camp A-555 dispensary learning from Green Beret medics the rudiments of first aid.

Miraculously the children had come through relatively unscathed. Beyond bumped heads and ugly purple bruises on their arms and legs, their main complaint was that they had been frightened out of their wits by the experience. One little girl, who looked to be about four years old, clutched a doll tightly in her arms. Her equivalent of a Barbie doll was a stern-featured Chinese woman with a red cape draped over her shoulders, which covered most of a long gold-and-green embroidered dress. The doll held a long stick with a lantern hanging from a string.

The old man sat up and beckoned for Morrow to approach. Both the sallow expression on his face, and his labored breathing betrayed the fact that he was in great pain. Grasped firmly in his gnarled hand was a cheap gold crucifix; the icon marked him as one of Vietnam's Catholics.

When Morrow finally saw his leg with the broken femur poking out of his thigh, she nearly vomited.

"How are you feeling, old man?" she asked in a soothing voice. She didn't expect him to be able to speak English, but hoped her gentle tone would reassure him and help assuage his pain.

He smiled. "I've had better days," he responded in perfect English. "As you can see, I've been knocked around a bit."

"Yes. But nothing's broken that can't be mended."

"Yes, I'm sure you're right," he answered without conviction.

While she cleaned and dressed the lesser wounds gouged into his arm and shoulders, he lay quietly before her, holding the crucifix with its chain wrapped tightly around his hand. He was torn up so badly there was only so much Morrow could do. Not wanting to try to reset the compound fracture, she enlisted One-Eye's help and the two of them immobilized it with a bamboo splint so that the sharp, splintered edges of the bone wouldn't do any more damage to the thigh muscle. Finished, she placed her hand on his and told him, "I've done all I can. I'm no doctor, but you really need to see one and have him fix that leg. You're seriously injured."

The old man started to laugh, but the laughter made him cough and grimace in pain. When he recovered, his voice was weaker. "This is Vietnam, not Chicago. There are no doctors within thirty kilometers." He held the crucifix close to his heart. "Out here we put our faith in God. There are no other choices," he intoned solemnly.

He looked very peaceful lying there in the corner of the hut. The pain seemed to leave his body; he breathed a sigh of relief and closed his eyes. Instantly One-Eye started babbling excitedly in Vietnamese. Morrow rested her finger against the old man's carotid artery and got no pulse. The old man was dead. Morrow's eyes felt watery as she murmured, "Out here we put our faith in God. Right."

By dawn her work was done. The hapless women and children had been attended to, given an herbal tea with medicinal properties and were soon sleeping. Relatives had come for the old man's body. They would wash and bury it.

Morrow and One-Eye stepped out of the hut and watched an NVA soldier squatting on the ground alongside an ant trail. These were leaf-cutter ants that tore hunks of greenery off bushes with their sharp pincers and then carried them back to their underground nests. Once the leaves became moldy, they ate the spores like mushrooms.

The NVA soldier had sprayed lighter fluid along the column of leaf-cutter ants who came and went from foliage to nest. The army of ants ignored the flammable liquid doused over their bodies and continued their relentless campaign against the shrubbery. The soldier pulled an American-made Zippo out of his pocket, struck a flame and touched it to the liquid. As the blaze fired up, he started laughing, dancing around and pointing as hundreds of ants went crazy running away from the heat and flames.

Morrow looked at One-Eye. The two of them looked at the sadistic soldier, then at the hut where the injured women and children lay sleeping. One-Eye nodded, stomped over to the soldier and kicked him in the seat of the pants, knocking him flat on his face. The man rolled over, looked up at One-Eye and started jabbering away in an angry voice. One-Eye responded by planting a foot on the man's chest and pointing an admonishing finger at him as he talked in a calm voice. The soldier, gulped, listened and nodded. After a while One-Eye let him up and he scurried away.

One-Eye escorted Morrow back to her hut. She wiped her bloodstained palm across her pant leg, smearing it across her thigh. She could still feel blood, dried and sticky, between the web of her fingers. "I'd never make a doctor. Just don't have the mind-set," said Morrow. "I don't like seeing anybody hurt. Especially children. I'm afraid I just don't have the stomach for this kind of work."

"I disagree," said One-Eye. "I watch. You did very good job." He put a hand on her shoulder and smiled. "You not worry. You go home soon."

FOR TWO DAYS after Morrow had tended the wounded Vietnamese, she and Maxwell had simply wandered around the village under the watchful eye of Dinh and One-Eye. On the third day Dinh told them they would be making a trip through the jungle.

Both Morrow and Maxwell realized there was nothing they could do but comply with the man's instructions. And so they had started walking.

Now, during a break, Dinh called Morrow and Maxwell close to his side. His usual easygoing personality had dissolved like a cube of sugar in hot coffee, and now his demeanor was as stern and as serious as that of a hangman.

"You are about to see the war firsthand. You are going to see something that may trouble you. At the very least it will cause you some consternation. Throughout this exercise your hands will remain unbound, but I must caution you. If you run, you will be shot. If you break silence, you will be shot. If you initiate any action by yourself, do anything you are not commanded to do, you will be shot. If one is guilty and the other innocent, both will be shot. Is all of that clear?"

Crystal clear, thought Morrow. Wherever they were going, and whatever it was they were about to do, there would be no latitude for screwing up.

Jerry Maxwell didn't like the sound of it. Frowning, he folded his arms across his chest. "Maybe we don't want to see what you're about to show us. Whatever it is you've got planned doesn't sound like my cup of tea."

Morrow gave her partner's arm a cautionary nudge and addressed the NVA officer. "I want you to answer frankly, Captain Dinh. Will we be in any danger?"

Dinh nodded. "Yes, great danger. But certainly no more than my own men who will accompany you. To put it bluntly, you could be killed even if you do exactly as you are told." He shrugged, "As you learned the other night when you bandaged the women and children who were injured in the B-52 raid, there are no guarantees in life."

"I see. Then let me ask whether we have any choice in the matter. Can we opt to pass on this experience?"

"No," Dinh said sternly. "You will accompany us. It has already been deemed necessary that you see this. You have no choice in the matter. This point is nonnegotiable."

"Okay," Maxwell grumbled. "It seems we have no choice. "Then I guess it's time to tell us what you've got planned for us. Where are we going and what are we going to do?"

"Maxwell," said Dinh.

"Yeah?"

Dinh responded in his best colloquial English. "Go pack sand up your ass."

Hours later, and in the heat of the day, Morrow heard them—helicopters off in the distance but closing fast. One-Eye grabbed his M-16 and shouted to the two Americans, telling them to stay out of sight. When Morrow didn't respond quickly enough, he ran over and roughly shoved her to the ground, knocking the wind out of her.

Heart beating madly, and struggling to catch her breath, Morrow crouched behind a thick tree, more for concealment than cover. She knew from experience that trees didn't always stop machine gun bullets, and they certainly wouldn't provide much protection against rockets.

The beating of the rotors grew louder. She could tell there was more than one in the flight, but she couldn't tell how many. From her cover Morrow couldn't see much of the sky but could hear the pounding of the rotors as the helicopters drew nearer. The sound peaked in intensity as they flew directly overhead, the wash shaking the treetops. After the sound faded, One-Eye got back to his feet and brushed off his clothing.

Seemingly shaken by the experience, he started babbling to Morrow that helicopters were the worst foe they faced, telling her how jet-powered F-4 Phantoms and prop-driven A-1 Skyraiders flew too high and turned too slowly to effectively make war on individual soldiers. But the highly feared helicopter could chase a man like a cat pursuing a mouse and kill him with machine gun or rocket fire.

They stood there in silence, just listening. In the distance they could hear gunfire where the Huey had randomly opened up with its machine guns. The technique was called reconnaissance by fire and consisted of trying to sucker the enemy into firing back and giving away his position. But Dinh's men were too well trained for that.

The signal came up the line to move. For an hour they continued walking through the tangle of vines that covered the slightly overgrown trail, until One-Eye pointed to a spot on the ground where a huge tree had been felled by lightning. He motioned for Morrow and Maxwell to lie down behind it, then he crouched down beside them. Peering over the top of the trunk, Morrow observed the rest of the NVA unit disperse among the natural camouflage of the jungle's trees and bushes. Then they waited.

After an hour of lying motionless, Morrow heard voices. At first she couldn't make them out, but as they came closer she detected the distinct speech patterns of a man with a Southern drawl expressing his need for a much-needed three-day pass to sample the fleshpots of Tu Do Street. "Good Lord willin' and the creek don't rise," chimed in a buddy, "I'm savin' my money for a brand-new Corvette with a 327 and dual quads."

One-Eye planted a sharp kick in Morrow's ribs and gave her a withering glance. She returned a hurt look, and saw him tap his index finger against the trigger guard of his AK-47. He stared directly into her eyes. She read the message loud and clear: keep your head down and your mouth shut, or die.

As the American unit approached, she could feel the tension closing in on her. In fact, she was surprised the Georgia boy on point hadn't sensed he was about to lead his squad into an ambush.

Morrow got One-Eye's attention, and using hand gestures, asked for permission to peer over the log. She didn't want to watch, and yet she knew she had to. He nodded his assent, but then corrected it, motioning her to look around the side of the log and not over the top. That made sense: peering around the side, she would cast a lower profile and was less likely to be spotted.

From her vantage point she saw three GIs in jungle fatigues carrying M-16s as they padded down the trail. The American soldiers were so close to her hideout she could smell the strange odor of after-shave mingled with mosquito repellent.

She turned to her right and looked fifty feet down the trail to where she knew an NVA soldier was hidden. The man's tiny brown hand slowly reached out from behind a boulder. In his grasp was an AK-47 banana clip. The NVA soldier adjusted the clip's position until a ray of sunlight reflected off the brass cartridges. There he held it, sparkling bright for all the world, and especially the point man, to see. Why would he do that? she wondered. Wasn't this an ambush? And the idea of an ambush was to surprise the enemy, wasn't it? If so, why tip off the GIs with the AK clip? Obviously they wanted the American patrol to spot it. But why?

It only took a minute. The Southerner shouted in an animated voice, "Ambush!" The hidden NVA soldier immediately let go of the telltale magazine and popped off a round. The squad dispersed, instinctively running away from the gunfire, down the side of the hill and taking cover behind the trees almost directly in front of Morrow and Maxwell.

The enemy soldier started taking potshots at the Americans, who in turn returned fire in long, wasteful bursts. One of the GIs warned his buddies, saying, "Grenade!" A moment later he pulled the pin on an M-26 fragmentation grenade and hurled it as hard and as far as he could in the direction of the soldier who had started the firefight. Five seconds later the sharp blast echoed hollowly through the jungle, the shrapnel scarring tree trunks, slashing through leaves, the sound of the blast scaring the monkeys. No more firing came from the NVA who had hidden behind the tree.

Morrow watched in disgust as only three of the twelve American soldiers actually engaged in the firefight. The rest simply rolled over and died. She had never seen real cowards under fire before and had personally been involved in a number of firefights and sieges alongside her Green Beret compatriots. But this time she looked on incredulously as two American infantrymen dropped their rifles, curled up in the fetal position and never fired a single round from their weapons. The other squad members feverishly fired off twenty-round magazines on full-auto without aiming.

Then Dinh sprang his trap. Behind the American position two NVA soldiers boldly stood and trained their weapons. "Hey, GI," one of them cried derisively, "you numbah one jungle fighter."

The two Americans who had been doing all the fighting whirled in time to see the AKs open up, cutting the exposed squad to ribbons. They killed the two young lions first because they were the most dangerous. Next they killed the simpering cowards because they despised them. Finally, after reloading, they riddled the rest of the American unit.

Once the AKs and the M-16s had fallen silent, the NVA walked among the dead and wounded Americans, kicking the bloodied bodies and finishing off the ones who were still breathing. Morrow plainly heard one of the wounded GIs cry out for his mother before one of Dinh's men put a bullet behind his left ear. Morrow closed her eyes and shuddered, imagining what it would have been like to die that way.

Stunned by the ambush, Morrow suddenly understood why the enemy soldier had twirled his AK magazine until it sparkled in the sunlight. He had wanted the American soldiers to see the reflection so that they'd run away from him and take cover on the reverse slope of the hill where his comrades would be waiting with open arms. Dinh had planned it this way; he knew exactly how the Americans would react.

The air was thick with the stench of spilled blood and automatic rifle fire. Morrow's stomach was queasy. To quell her nausea, she rested a hand on the log. Spotting her predicament, One-Eye grabbed her by the chin and stared at her. "You okay?" he asked, concerned about her health. "You be sick. It okay with me." In words and gestures he went on to tell her how he had been sick to his stomach the first time they had wiped out an American unit by trickery, but after seeing the carnage a B-52 strike could wreak on a village, he never again felt pity for the soldiers.

Using One-Eye's canteen, Morrow rinsed her mouth, spitting a stream of water onto the ground. Feeling better, she considered whether or not she should look at the young American bodies with their faces and stomaches torn up by bullets. Somehow she felt it was her duty, although she didn't understand why. She turned to Maxwell, whose face was ashen.

"Why?" she asked him. "Why did Dinh run this ambush? Was this like the C-rations he fed us the other night? Did he just do it to show us he could? What's the sense in all this?"

By now Maxwell's color was returning, and he wasn't sure whether his emotion was rage or sorrow. "There's no sense in war, Robin. And I don't think they did this especially for us. This is what these people do. This is what our people do. This is war, ugly, fucking war, not a goddamn gentleman's duel with pistols at twenty paces."

"But it wasn't fair...."

Maxwell didn't answer for a while. He just stared at her. "Yeah. It isn't fair. So?"

The two of them looked on as the NVA soldiers hurriedly flipped the dead onto their backs, unlaced and yanked off jungle boots and jammed them onto their own feet in place of Ho Chi Minh sandals.

One VC whooped and hollered when he found a compass. Another showed off an extremely revealing snapshot of a dead GI's girlfriend. A dozen Vietnamese crowded around the photo, giggling in their high-pitched voices and pointing at the woman's naked body.

Maxwell saw what was going on and knew they were all fantasizing having sex with the dead GI's girlfriend. The CIA man smiled at them and muttered under his breath, "She wouldn't fuck any one of you guys even if you were a foot taller, a million dollars richer and had a dick the size of a tree trunk."

Without warning, the VC with the picture pulled away from the huddle. Still holding the photo in one hand, he pulled out his penis and started to urinate on the dead GI's face. Dinh saw him and yelled, startling him so thoroughly he ended up urinating all over himself. Shamefaced, the VC ran off into the jungle, ignoring the taunts of his friends.

The intelligence officer went through the dead GI's personal effects, looking for maps. Not interested in geographical data—the NVA had good maps of their own—he searched instead for troop locations and unit designations that might have been grease-penciled onto the clear plastic overlay of a map. If found, such information would provide the NVA with hard intelligence data. And Maxwell knew if they turned up anything, there wasn't a damn thing he could do.

Dinh walked around the scene of the battle, his somber mood still with him. He nodded his approval as he surveyed the carnage, shouting compliments to his men for pulling off the ambush. As he shouted individual endorsements to each man in turn, the man would humbly smile, nod and give a terse reply.

Then Dinh addressed Maxwell. "Your soldiers fired *beaucoup* ammunition, maybe two, three thousand rounds, and detonated one hand grenade. My men fired less than one hundred bullets. From your soldiers we have captured an M-60 machine gun, eleven worthless M-16 rifles, two thousand rounds of ammunition and twelve hand grenades. American imperialists manufacture lousy rifles, but very good hand grenades."

Dinh and the two Americans looked on in silence as some of the NVA soldiers strode past carrying a makeshift litter with a body on it. Morrow recognized it as the man who had triggered the ambush. His face and chest were covered with blood, and fingers were missing on his right hand. "Is he dead?" she asked.

Dinh commented. "Not yet. Unfortunately for his wife and children, we will lose another good soldier within the hour."

"How many dead Americans?" asked Morrow.

"Twelve," he answered impassively.

Maxwell summoned up the nerve to ask a question, a question whose answer he wasn't sure he wanted to hear. "Does this happen often? I mean, are most American soldiers this much of a pushover?"

"No," Dinh said. "Some soldiers have dogs—you call them German shepherds. Scout dogs sniff us out before we can spring my trap. Cause problems. They see, hear and smell where GIs blind and deaf, stumbling and fumbling."

Morrow stared straight into Dinh's eyes. "This was a slaughter, plain and simple."

He looked at her as if she were mad. "No sense in getting into battle if you do not have the firepower on your side. This way saves many lives. All you do this way is pick over the dead American bodies, and you do not have to carry your own dead home." With that, Dinh walked away, leaving Morrow and Maxwell alone.

Maxwell watched Dinh walk away, then nudged Morrow. "He understands, Robin."

"Understands what, for Chrissakes?"

"The value of a secret weapon."

"Are you back on that crap again? I thought you got it out of your system back at the Saigon Rose."

"He understood the value of a secret weapon when he fed us U.S. government C-rations, when he showed us how scary it is to see two hundred rocks or bullets coming straight at your face, and just now, when he showed us he can wipe out an American patrol as easy as pie. He knows that if you write about any of this stuff, it'll demoralize the readers on the homefront. You see, if the public doesn't know about Dinh, he's a secret weapon. The Communist cause needs you, Robin. They're not going to win without you."

"What are you saying, Jerry? I'm not in the mood for riddles. Whatever's on your mind, spit it out, or damn well shut up."

"Like the socialists say, whatever is, is. And the fact is, if you write about this stuff, you're aiding and abetting the enemy. When and if we get back, I'm going to advise you to keep your mouth shut about everything we've seen. It's in the best interest of our national security. If all those eighteen-year-old draftees read about what we've seen, they're going to go to Canada in droves. And it will be your fault."

"First of all, Maxwell. Whatever I write is my business, not yours. And secondly, it's a free country, and if some misguided kid goes to Canada, it's not my problem or yours. So, like the man said, go pack a handful of sand where it will do the most good."

11

IN THE JUNGLE NEAR
ELEPHANT EAR
CAMBODIA

As the dust of battle began to settle, Fetterman realized he had been separated from the rest of his A-team; Gerber and the others were nowhere to be found. Since a reassembly point hadn't been specified in the heat of battle, it was unlikely he would be able to link up with Gerber and the others. Blind dumb luck wouldn't be very likely to bless him, either, the way things were going.

Even worse, he was without a compass or a map, two tools essential to navigation in the jungle. He was on his own and would have to figure his way out of the predicament solo. If not, he would either be captured by the enemy and risk sitting out the duration of the war in a POW camp, or simply die from hunger, thirst or disease. None of these alternatives appealed to him much.

From high atop the nameless hill where he stood pondering his situation, Fetterman could see across the stretch of broad green valley that lay before him. Above the hazy blue horizon the sun radiated pulses of light and intense heat. He wiped his sleeve across his forehead, seemingly soaking up the sweat with the shirt fabric. It was one hot mother, he mused. Squinting, he held his hand out as if to shield his eyes against the glare, but instead he was calculating how long before sunset, using the number of fingers between the horizon and the sun. He had learned that each finger represented fifteen minutes. "Time," he said out loud. Fourteen hundred hours, seven in the morning, midnight—words and numbers made mortal man feel secure, helped uncivilized man to cling to the notion of civilization.

Fetterman thought about the dog-eating Montagnards he had broken bread with the previous day. Other than the joy or pain of the moment, time didn't matter to a Stone Age tribesman. If a sports fan tried to whip a Montagnard into a frenzy over the fact that one Olympic runner could run a mile a hundredth of a second faster than the next fastest athlete, the Montagnard would simply stare at the sports fan as if he were mad.

A Montagnard wouldn't be able to comprehend the notion of a hundredth of a second, and even if such a concept was adequately explained, he'd wonder why it mattered whether one man was infinitesimally faster than another. And why the hurry in the first place? Why run when you can walk?

Fetterman figured in the final analysis the Montagnards' attitude toward life was correct. When one really got down to what mattered in the world, civilized man's concept of seconds and minutes and hours was meaningless. In the jungle all that mattered was how much time was left until sunset turned the world black. And that related directly to Fetterman's current situation: he had to cover as much ground as he could before the lights went out. And standing there philosophizing, he was burning daylight.

Fetterman decided to move on. Without a compass, a map or any readily definable landmarks in the jungle, he was in dire straits. Extracting himself from his difficult situation would require common sense, savvy and patience. All were qualities he was blessed with. From the position of the sun he was able to roughly calculate east. He knew marching in the general direction would at least move him toward Vietnam. Admittedly it was a long shot, but worth the risk, he figured.

Facing that direction, he lined up a set of three trees and started walking. When he got to the first tree, he lined up three more with the second tree now the first and so on. This method would at least keep him moving in a straight line and an easterly direction, and without it he would likely walk around in a great circle, exhausting his energy and wasting time. As long as he kept moving east, he would be okay. Even if he had to walk the entire width of South Vietnam, he would eventually bump into an American unit or the South China Sea. With any luck, he would escape and evade his way out. No problem, he kept telling himself. No problem.

HOURS PASSED as the day turned into night. Fetterman decided to take a break. Sitting with his back against a tree, he closed his eyes and tried to sleep, knowing that even a five- or ten-minute catnap would refresh him. His stomach grumbled. He wished he'd eaten more back at the camp. The wieners and beans would have tasted good about now, he mused as his mouth started watering. I'm not hungry, he told himself.

A mosquito buzzed his ear. He slapped it away, then reached down to rub his legs. The muscles ached from his trek through the jungle. His scabbed forearm throbbed painfully where the bullet had torn away a piece of his flesh. Although it had stopped bleeding, the untreated wound worried him. In the jungle, without antibiotics, the wound would certainly become infected in a day or two. And if he didn't get it taken care of soon thereafter, it seemed reasonable to conclude he might lose the arm to gangrene.

He started counting the throbbing pulse in his injured arm, thinking about the Montagnards again. He recalled the time when he, Gerber and Dirty Shirt Crawley had been in one of the Montagnard's thatched hut villages up in the Central Highlands on an intelligence-gathering mission. VC had been in the area and the S-2 types needed to know the enemy strength in accurate numbers. Therefore Captain Gerber had asked the village chief how many VC officers he had seen. The chief had held up three fingers and said, "Three."

"And how many heavy mortars?"

The chief had held up a single finger and said, "One."

"How many soldiers?"

The chief had thrust out ten fingers and said, "Many."

At that point Dirty Shirt Crawley had spoken to the chief in his native tongue, then relayed his finding to Gerber. "They don't have a word in their language that goes that high, Captain. But I have an idea." Dirty Shirt had handed the chief a stick and asked him to make tick marks in the dirt, one tick mark for every VC soldier.

The chief had taken the stick and bantered back and forth with the other men in the village. After a while he had begun scratching marks in the dirt. When he was finished, he'd handed the stick back to Gerber. The captain and Fetterman had each counted fifty-seven tick marks. The chief had smiled proudly, again held up ten fingers and said, "Many."

Fetterman drifted off to sleep, reflecting on a people who were so poor they didn't even have a number higher than ten. They rarely saw that many of anything, except rice, and all you needed to describe *beaucoup* rice was the word *many*.

Sometime later he awoke, feeling a weight on his chest. Darkness had fallen, and he couldn't see what it was. Probably a big jungle rat, he assumed. If he startled it, it might feel cornered and bite him in self-defense. That wouldn't be a pleasant experience, and at the very least he would have yet another infection to deal with, if not rabies. Keeping calm, he snapped out his right hand and grabbed the hairy thing on his chest, flinging it as hard as he could. Then he started laughing. "You're one bright guy, Sergeant Fetterman. What would Mack think if he knew your arm fell asleep on your chest and you thought it was a goddamn rodent?"

Then he heard a faint sound echoing off the tree trunks, a sound so faint and so distant it was nearly drowned out by the whirring and buzzing of the bugs. And even though the noise emanated from far off in the jungle, the fact that the humming originated from a portable electrical generator was unmistakable. The steady throbbing of the engines carefully regulated to never fluctuate up or down from eighteen hundred RPMs in order to produce 240 volts of a constant sixty cycles gave it a voice all its own.

Even more important than the source of the sound was the fact that it meant the presence of a sizable American contingent within earshot of him. Within earshot, he thought. Big deal. The jungle could play tricks on a man. The camp could be as close as a hundred yards away or ten miles distant. Either way, he had no other choice but to track it down.

Eyelids twitching from fatigue and leg muscles stiff from the exertion of having walked countless miles and then being teased by a few hours' rest, Fetterman plodded toward the sound.

An hour later he lay flat on his belly at the edge of the tree line, staring at an American encampment under a full moon. Fetterman felt like a mountain lion that had been on the prowl, roaming the trails that went up into the jungle-clad mountains and down into the fog-shrouded valleys. Like a mountain lion stumbling across the intrusions of civilized man into the wilds, he studied the encampment.

Beyond the tree line lay the wide-open ground of the killing zone. About three hundred yards of trees and brush had already been cleared away. From the smell of freshly turned earth permeating the air, and the fact that there was no perimeter wire, he decided the men had arrived sometime earlier that day.

Beyond the killing field he spotted a sprinkling of sandbagged machine gun and mortar emplacements. In the center of the compound stood a large stone house, which had probably had its roof blown off, given the neighborhood. That made this encampment a new fire support base, so new in fact that it was still under construction. What blind luck, he thought.

Still giving the camp the once-over, he spotted the black profile of a water buffalo, a water tank big enough to be mounted on a trailer hooked up to a deuce-and-a-half. With a throat as dry as sand, he could almost smell the water conveniently parked near the mess hall and squad tents. These guys had it pretty easy, he figured, beginning to feel anger welling up inside. Straight legs ate hot food, never went thirsty and always slept on cots. Hootch maids shined their boots and swept out their huts. It was nothing less than the life of a colonial master and servants. Green Berets mostly ate cold C-rations, went without water and slept in a cramped jungle hammock hung between two trees in the middle of a cloud of mosquitoes.

Without even thinking, Fetterman began to crawl toward the compound, carefully feeling the ground in front of him for trip wires, patting the ground for concave depressions with soil packed over the top. An hour later he had negotiated the killing field and was midway between two sandbag emplacements.

The night was silent, save for the raucous whine of the GenSet. Moments later Fetterman worked his way into the heart of the compound and lay prone at the door of the big mess tent. He looked to either side. Seeing no one, he got to his feet, brushed the dirt off the palms of his hand and walked into the big tent as if he were the first sergeant.

There were a couple of long tables and chairs arranged in military fashion. A single light bulb burned overhead, pulsing brighter and dimmer with the revving of the GenSet. He could smell the pungent aroma of coffee but couldn't spot where it was kept. On top of one of the tables he found an aluminum pan filled with chocolate chip cookies. He picked one up; it felt warm in his hand. Now he was even angrier. Fresh fucking cookies!

Out of sheer anger he grabbed a cookie, opened his mouth and savagely attacked it, swallowing it in two bulging mouthfuls. He stared at the panful of cookies and began to eat them one at a time. Soon all that remained were the crumbs scattered along the bottom of the shiny pan. He burped, lay down at the foot of the table, snuggled close to his M-16 and went to sleep.

Fetterman didn't know how much time had passed when he heard footfalls on the ground outside. He cracked an eyelid in time to see a black soldier come into the tent. The soldier's complexion was so thoroughly black that his skin radiated a blue sheen. Garbed in fatigue pants, OD T-shirt and a white apron draped across his front, he was obviously a spoon, an Army cook showing up to prepare breakfast for the pampered leg unit. Fetterman closed his eyes again and lay perfectly still. Leg assholes, he thought to himself. We'll see where this goes.

The cook spotted Fetterman and stopped dead in his tracks. He stood there mouth agape for a couple of moments without moving, then whirled and trotted out of the tent.

A couple of minutes later he returned in the company of a young first lieutenant. From the looks of his tailored jungle fatigues, the lieutenant gave the appearance of having broken starch just for the occasion. His name tag spelled out: Carrington. Fetterman did notice Lieutenant Carrington wore a pair of subdued jump wings over his left shirt pocket. At least he wasn't a leg.

Fetterman got to his feet, pulled on his green beret and saluted. "Good morning, sir," he said.

Carrington returned the salute, then stared at the apparition that had crawled into his outpost from the jungle. Here was this Green Beret, with a blend of dirt and remnants of camouflage paint smeared across his stubbled face. With his knees and elbows torn out of his fatigues, the man looked as if he had been in a fight with a tiger. But the look in his eyes was what scared the young lieutenant the most. "Who are you and what are you doing here?" he asked.

Fetterman rocked back on his heels. Long ago he had learned to listen more to a man's tone of voice than the actual words that passed through his lips. To listen to the nearly indiscernible thread of emotion that hung on the edges of words told more than the words themselves. And so it seemed that what was really bothering the lieutenant was the fact that Fetterman had walked into his camp and no one had spotted him. And that meant Victor Charlie could have done the same thing. "Master Sergeant Fetterman, Fifth Special Forces. Separated from my detachment in the middle of a firefight, heard your GenSet singing its song, knew it meant Americans."

Carrington nodded as if he understood. "Well, listen, we're due to serve up some scrambled eggs, bacon and OJ in a few minutes. Hope you'll join us. You can eat with me and Colonel Staley, the CO." He turned to the cook. "Isn't that right, Snowflake?"

"Yes, sir," said Snowflake, who had obviously drawn his name because of the color of his skin. The nickname meant he was well liked.

Carrington brightened. "And you can tell us how you snuck in without alerting the guards."

Breakfast? Fetterman's spirts sank. Suddenly the cookies in his belly felt as if they weighed ten pounds and were getting heavier and heavier with each heartbeat. Gritting his teeth, he thought to himself, Outsmarted yourself, didn't ya, Tony? You ate cookies when you could have eaten real food—bacon and eggs. He smiled weakly and responded to the lieutenants offer of hospitality. "Wouldn't want to cut into your rations...."

Snowflake shrugged. "There's plenty. We usually end up throwing most of it away. Or sharing it with the zips. Some of those mamasans got lots of kids and no papasans to look out for them."

Fetterman decided in the interests of diplomacy that he could at least pick at the food. He forced a smile. "I'd be pleased to share your food."

"Good," said Carrington. "After breakfast we'll get on the radio and see what we can do about getting you linked up with your people. We've got a supply chopper scheduled in for tomorrow sometime. You should be able to hitch a ride."

With a practiced move intended to impress the SFer, Carrington turned on his heel and left. "Places to go, people to see," he muttered on his way out.

Fetterman and Snowflake exchanged glances. Then they both shrugged. "He's not so bad," said Snowflake.

Fetterman nodded. "So you going to offer me a cup of coffee or what?"

Snowflake nodded. "I make damn good coffee. Got a secret ingredient that enhances the flavor."

"Oh, yeah? What, you piss in it or something?" asked Fetterman good-naturedly.

Snowflake grimaced. "Sweet Jesus, man, no. I wouldn't piss in anybody's coffee. That would be a horrible thing to do to a man first thing in the morning." A smile slowly began to creep across his face. "But sometimes I do piss on the officer's bacon. Strange thing is, on those days they complain like a motherfucker that the bacon's too damn salty. Imagine that."

"Uh-huh. When I have breakfast with you guys," said Fetterman, "I'll be eating with the enlisted pukes."

Snowflake pointed at Fetterman's bloodied shirt sleeve.

"No damage done," replied Fetterman tersely.

Snowflake jerked his head, "C'mon, let's go wake that lazy-assed medic and have him dress your wound."

12

SOMEWHERE IN THE JUNGLE CAMBODIA

Huddled under the frilly protection of an Army-issue mosquito net, Sergeant Kimber T. Walsh manned the AN/PRC-74 radio. Earphones draped over the back of his head, he mindlessly listened to the irritating crackle of the airwaves on the ten MHZ band and dutifully swatted blood-sucking mosquitoes. As the junior commo man, he'd been the unlucky one, drawing radio watch from 2:00 a.m. until 4:00 a.m. He was passing the time wondering what fate had befallen Fetterman.

Walsh's brain cells were beginning to feel numb and his eyelids drooped. With a start, he jerked back his head and checked his wristwatch. As if on cue, he reached down to sweep the frequency dial across the band to the Australian Broadcasting Corporation where he'd be able to catch the world news and latest rock and roll music on the charts. The brief diversion would wake him up, he figured, then he'd swing back to the assigned frequency. As he began to tune in the station, he noticed a strange monotone.

The radio signal was coming through loud and clear, sounding as if it were very near. He'd been hearing it ever since they had deployed on the mission. At first he figured it was probably due to some freak atmospheric condition, and he had decided to ignore the aberration. But they had covered a lot of klicks since that first day, and the signal strength was still as strong as it had been the first time they'd heard it. Strange. Very strange. He found the Australian station and settled back to enjoy the sound of a human voice.

Walsh listened without much interest to the gravel-voiced news commentator until he heard the item about Robin Morrow. "Sweet Jesus!" he exclaimed, peeling off the earphones. Captain Gerber had to be told for personal reasons as well as the fact that the information related directly to the mission.

Throwing back the protection of the mosquito net, he hurried over to Gerber's jungle hammock. He knew that if he startled Gerber, the captain might overreact and come up with a knife drawn, so Walsh stood at the captain's feet, trying to figure out a way of waking him without undue alarm. After all, in the Army a man was considered potentially insane for the first thirty seconds after coming out of a deep slumber. Walsh didn't want to be mistaken for an NVA soldier. Standing at Gerber's feet, he called out in a quiet voice, "Captain, it's Walsh. Wake up."

Gerber immediately sat up. "I'm awake, Walsh. What is it?"

The RTO paused before answering. Taking a deep breath, he blurted, "Bad news, I'm afraid. I was monitoring the Aussie shortwave station. They say they've found the bodies of a Caucasian man and woman by the side of the road in Cambodia. They're pretty sure the dead people are Maxwell and Morrow."

Gerber didn't say anything for a while, which wasn't surprising given the circumstances. If the news broadcast was correct, it would cap a very bad day.

Gerber's longtime friend, Sergeant Fetterman, had presumably been killed or captured during the afternoon firefight, and now his captured girlfriend had been brutally tortured and her dead body dumped by the side of the road across the border from Cambodia. Yes, it was turning out to be a very bad day for the good guys.

Gerber finally said something to Walsh, his voice surprisingly calm. "Two things," he told the radioman. "First, there's nothing we can do about anything until morning. Second, you said they didn't positively ID Morrow as dead."

"That's right," said Walsh. "Like I said, the way they phrased it, it didn't sound like an absolutely positive ID. The faces were pretty torn up."

Gerber nodded. "They think it's her body, given the general description of the corpse. And while it's a long shot that it's not her, it could be some other Caucasian female. In short, we don't know any more now than we did before, except that a white woman's been murdered in Southeast Asia and—"

Gerber's train of logic was interrupted by the snap of a twig. Instinctively Walsh whirled to stare into the broad, smiling face of Chuyen. The radioman decided he didn't like the cold expression frozen on the Oriental's face.

Chuyen nodded at the two Americans, the gesture serving as a greeting. "Bad news come on radio, no?"

For the moment Gerber ignored Chuyen. "Walsh, I want you to encrypt a query and establish contact with the SFOB. Have them verify what you just told me. Put a rush on it."

"You got it," said Walsh, spinning on his heel.

"Chuyen," said Gerber. He paused for a moment before continuing. "Get your ass back in your hammock. I don't have time for you right now."

Thirty seconds after Gerber had given instructions, Walsh was back under his mosquito net shelter, crypto pad in hand, composing a message. Once that was done he tuned the transmitter for maximum signal strength and sent a blind transmission.

Before Gerber's A-team had deployed, they had established an arrangement whereby the Special Forces Operation Base at Nha Trang would listen for any communication from them on an assigned frequency for twenty-four hours a day. Whenever they made contact, the SFOB would compose a response and send it ten minutes later on an entirely different frequency. That way, if the enemy's Russian-trained high-speed Morse code intercept operators were lucky, or skillful enough to compromise one of the A-team's messages, they'd have to be twice as good to get the SFOB's reply.

After sending his message, Walsh started flipping the knob toward the frequency where the SFOB would answer. Midway there he heard a strange whine in the earphones. There it was again, the same loud, strange whine at precisely the same frequency. A light bulb went off in Walsh's head, and he hurriedly composed a second message and burned up the wires sending it off to Nha Trang. Finally he flipped to the assigned frequency and waited for the reply. If his wild-ass hunch was right about the source of that strange whine, things were about to get very hot, very fast.

INSIDE THE VAULT at the radio research facility near Nha Trang, they had nicknamed Sergeant Van Hook the Drone because once he had locked you into conversation he would go on and on about stock car racing, water beds, the evils of marijuana, how to make moonshine, how he had sent in ten dollars and was now an ordained minister or how he was going to reenlist and spend the ten-thousand-dollar bonus in a Bangkok whorehouse.

Drone was an enigma. His 201 personnel file said he was in Army intelligence, but he wasn't paid, assigned to duty stations or promoted by the Army. He worked for the Army Security Agency, a military branch of the National Security Agency.

The top page of his medical record was an eight-by-eleven sheet of paper with a stern warning that if Staff Sergeant "Drone" was ever wounded in combat, or involved in a car wreck back in the World, he was under no circumstances to be given painkillers or sedatives unless an ASA monitor was present. Because under their narcotic influence, Drone might unknowingly babble about critical intelligence and compromise the uncompromisable. But if a monitor was at least there to take notes on what he said, the surgical/medical staff could be debriefed and required to sign the necessary paperwork.

Sitting at his gray metal desk, Drone patted his paunch, burped, pushed back his black-rimmed glasses and went back to studying the data sent in from the radio research field stations at Phu Bai and Ban Me Thuoc.

This particular radio research mission had involved the intercept of a monotone transmission at 12127 megahertz. It had only taken a minute for the 05 Delta operators at the outposts and locally at Nha Trang to blend the directional antennae with compass rose and map in order to cut, plot and fix the location of the phantom radio sending the monotone radio signal. And now, without a doubt, they knew where it originated, having electronically pinned down the grid coordinates to within one hundred square meters.

Drone picked up the phone and called the Green Berets at the other end of the compound.

Someone picked up the receiver on the first ring. "Sergeant Jones, and this isn't a secure line. Can I help you, sir?" His voice had the sound of a very confident man.

"Staff Sergeant Van Hook over at the 403d Radio Research Group. Hook up your KY-7 ASAP." Drone had already plugged in his military-issue scrambler. He was about to pass along vital information, and he didn't want any eavesdropping enemy agents to benefit from it. Drone considered himself extremely security-conscious.

"Done," responded Jones. Drone could tell from the tinny sound of the Green Beret's voice that the KY-7 was in place and functioning properly.

"You wondered about that signal up around 12 megahertz . . . ?"

"Yeah," Jones said. "We got a rush on it. Got an A-team in the field more than a little anxious. Like everybody else hounding you guys, we need it yesterday. Lives may depend on it."

"Yeah, well, when you put in the request for it, you gave us the grid coordinates of your team, wondering how far apart they were from the transmission. You sitting down, Sergeant Jones? This is heavy shit."

Jones figured the guy must like the sound of his own voice. "Forget the history lesson and quit fucking around. Just give me the goddamn coordinates, or I'm going to walk over there and yank your head off."

"It's coming from their location. The fix on the monotone matched the team's coordinates, one and the same. We also ran a radio fingerprint on the transmitter. Consensus around here is that the signal is a low-power homing beacon. I'd say you've got a traitor with that A-team. Even worse, it means the NVA know exactly where your boys are, to within three hundred feet or so. Well, except for one of the NVA who's probably drinking coffee and shooting the shit with your boys right now. Hell, who knows? Maybe what they ought to do—"

Jones hung up and instantly redialed the commo shack. Minutes later the SFOB was on the air.

THE SUDDEN FLURRY of Morse code coming across the earphones at twenty groups per minute startled Walsh. He had nearly fallen asleep waiting for Nha Trang to get back to him. Pencil in hand, he transposed Morse code characters into alpha notation. When the transmission ended, he decrypted the ciphers by transposing cipher text into clear text. When he read the message aloud, there was a sinking feeling in the pit of his stomach. "Fuck," he murmured. "Holy fuck!"

He threw back his mosquito net and started over to tell Gerber the news. But before he had taken two steps he ran smack into Chuyen.

"Ah, Sergeant Walsh," whispered Chuyen. "I watch you. You good radioman. Very smart. More bad news come over radio?"

Before Walsh could reply, Chuyen made his move, grabbing Walsh's collar on either side of his neck. With his wrists crossed, he pulled the edges of the collar tight, effectively shutting off the supply of blood to Walsh's brain. Walsh hung there, boots kicking in thin air, trying to breathe, trying to scream. But Chuyen's combat judo hold had cut off the commo man's wind and the supply of blood to his brain. Moments later, when Walsh's head sagged, Chuyen let him drop to the ground. Chuyen knew the American might still be alive, but he didn't have the time to check. The Oriental got on his hands and knees and began searching for the commo pad Walsh had dropped.

Suddenly Krung's voice rang out in the night. "Why you kill Walsh, Chuyen? Him not bad fellow for American. Him good buddy. Like to kill VC."

Calmly Chuyen got to his feet, brushing off his knees. "He not dead. Just sleep. Not have time to kill. Must go. You not try to stop.'' Chuyen heard the rasping sound of Krung pulling his knife out of his sheath.

''You not try to go,'' countered Krung.

Chuyen growled low in his throat and charged. Krung just stood there. At the last possible moment he stepped to one side, and with a deft sideways motion, swept his knife toward Chuyen's chin.

The traitor hurtled past for two or three steps before he ran out of steam. Protectively holding his hand against the side of his neck, he turned around to face Krung.

''Now try shaking head,'' Krung rasped.

Chuyen fell to his knees. In the moonlight Krung could see the bigger man working his mouth, but no words issued from his lips, only a strange wheezing noise and a lot of blood. A moment later he toppled forward onto his face.

Knife in hand, Krung started toward Chuyen, then stopped dead in his tracks. He sheathed the knife, whirled and trotted over toward Walsh. Now conscious, the radioman was trying to sit up.

''Chuyen. Chuyen,'' said Walsh in a hoarse voice.

''Him dead. I kill.''

''Gerber. Get Captain Gerber. We're in deep *kimchee*.''

13

NATIONAL AIRPORT
WASHINGTON, D.C.

The morning after Johnson's funeral, Dirty Shirt Crawley packed his duffel bag and caught a cab from Nebraska Hall to National Airport. Once he checked his luggage with the skycap, he headed for the rest room. Relieving himself at the urinal, he zippered his fly, turned and started toward the door, passing a stern-faced Marine PFC who stood at the sink washing his hands. "In the Corps," the Marine derisively called out, "We always wash our hands after we piss."

Without missing a beat, Dirty Shirt said flatly, "Who fucking rah, Mac. In the Special Forces we don't dribble all over our hands when we take a leak." Flabbergasted by the reply, the Marine groped for a comeback, but before his mind was able to grab hold of an appropriate reply, Dirty Shirt was out the door and gone.

"Fucking jarhead," Shirt muttered, stalking down the long hallway. With his stomach growling loud enough to wake the dead, he wandered into the terminal, which was filled with rows of chairs. Most of the ones he walked past were empty, the rows briefly reminding him of the headstones in Arlington National Cemetery and Johnson's burial ceremony.

Dirty Shirt stared at the chairs in disgust. Such chairs were one of the reasons he hated airports. Wryly he observed these were plastic with stainless-steel armrests designed so a weary traveler could never find comfort in them, let alone lie down and sleep during a twelve-hour layover. And, of course, the rationale for such monstrosities was the fact that airport management didn't want to encourage street people to find refuge at the airport. Air traveler be damned.

Continuing through the terminal he noticed an elderly woman, seemingly without direction or purpose, change course in midstream in order to intersect his path. Her blue hair was well coiffed in some ancient style and her earrings were as big as Ford Thunderbird hubcaps. She wore an oversize blue-and-white cotton dress that reminded him of something his late grandmother had once worn.

Shirt figured the lady standing in front of him needed directions to the TWA flights. Or maybe she wanted to know where she could get a bite to eat. He decided he'd help if he could. Already he felt a warm glow welling up inside of him. He felt like a Boy Scout about to do his good deed for the day.

Now, face-to-face with the strapping Green Beret, the woman smiled at him as if he were her son. "Pardon me, can I ask you a question?" Her smile looked sweet and kind.

"Sure," he said.

The transformation happened so quickly that it took Dirty Shirt completely by surprise. In a split second the lady's face went from near angelic to demonic. The carotid veins bulged in her neck and threatened to burst. The wrinkles in her forehead furrowed in an obvious expression of anger. Her jaw clenched so tightly that Dirty Shirt wondered how she was even able to get the words out without breaking her teeth.

"Do you mind telling me what you think you're doing over there in Vietnam, you murdering animal?"

Mouth agape, Dirty Shirt instinctively took a step backward.

She stepped nearer, closing the distance, and continued with her merciless tirade. Waving her index finger in front of his nose as if it were a big stick, she whipped at him with fingertip and words. "Why in God's holy name are you killing all those innocent women and children? How can you sleep at night? How can you live with yourself, you evil man? You should be ashamed of your war crimes, you baby killer. You drug addict. You drug-crazed murdering bastard. How would you like it if the Communists came over here and just started running around killing innocent women and children? Well, how would you?"

He bit his tongue and murmured to himself, "If they started with you, I'd like it just fine."

He didn't think that it was fair for the old woman to personally blame him for every aspect of the war. It didn't matter her facts weren't straight. It was as if he, Dirty Shirt Crawley, had personally dreamed up the war and pulled the trigger or napalmed every dead zip. And all that just for kicks. How could he respond to such an attack by an ignorant woman? No matter how he explained his part in all of it, she wouldn't listen, she wouldn't hear his words.

He wondered what she would think if he told her how the VC murdered fathers, disemboweled pregnant mothers and beheaded six-year-old girls just to make a point. And would she care to hear about how the Cong castrated GIs they captured and then sewed their genitals inside their mouths?

He figured none of it mattered. The old woman's mind was made up and closed tightly against any opinion other than her own. She wasn't asking him a question and then patiently waiting for an answer. She was telling him how it was from her point of view, the only point of view on the face of the earth that had any merit. In his estimation she was one of those people who heard what they wanted to hear and disregarded the rest. The way he figured it, there was absolutely nothing he could say to change her mind, nothing he could do to even get her to listen to his point of view. There was nothing to do but turn and walk away.

He left her standing there, yelling and screaming after him. Thankfully she didn't follow. With every step he took, the sound of her voice faded more and more into the distance. But his heart still pounded from the confrontation.

And then he saw the two hippies, a lanky kid and his girlfriend. Both of them looked to be in their early twenties. The guy was sporting the Jesus Christ look with long hair and beard, his white cotton peasant shirt embroidered with fancy red and blue butterflies. A big peace medallion hung by a leather thong around his neck. Shirt figured the hippie chick had probably sewn them on for him one night while they were sitting around smoking marijuana.

Her hair was long, brown and oily. Her peasant shirt was of white cotton and devoid of any embroidery. She had poured herself into a pair of dirty blue jeans. The two hippies sat on the floor, backs against the wall. Wedged in beside them were two soiled backpacks with bedrolls lashed to the top.

Dirty Shirt doubted whether the flimsy packs would hold up even a day in the jungle. As he walked past, the two kids started to sing a song and point at him with their grubby fingers. "GI Joe. GI Joe. Fighting man who can't beat Uncle Ho. Baby Killer. Murderer. Who'd you kill today? Hey, hey, hey."

Forcing himself to grin, the Green Beret stopped dead in his tracks, lowered himself onto his haunches and began to stare directly into the Jesus Christ look-alike's soft brown eyes. Dirty Shirt was so close to him that he thought he was going to gag on the strong scent of patchouli oil. Suddenly the two kids quit singing their stupid song. Shirt continued to stare. For a moment the hippie tried to match his gaze. Then, wriggling like a fish on dry land, he blinked and looked away. The girl took her man's hand and pressed it into her own. Suddenly the hippies were pretending the Green Beret didn't even exist.

Dirty Shirt imagined himself back at Nha Trang recondo school pushing ARVN troops, and reveled in the thought of having the hippie in his platoon where he could run him to death, or at least until the bastard fell to the ground, puking his guts out onto the red soil.

Dirty Shirt nodded and stood up. "So much for the courage of your conviction. Guys like you remind me of a schoolyard bully. Big mouths, no guts. Stand up to you, go face-to-face and you turn into a whimpering puddle of piss."

Shirt remembered how the sergeant at Nebraska Hall had told him about peaceniks in downtown D.C. ripping off GIs' campaign ribbons and CIBs. He looked at the peace medallion and considered revenge. Instead, he chose to control his wrath and continue on his way.

After what seemed about twenty miles of corridor and a thousand rows of plastic and chrome chairs, he found what resembled a cafeteria. He recognized it from the stainless-steel counters, and the caldrons of food bubbling away behind waist-high glass windows.

Someone who couldn't spell correctly had taped signs onto the glass in front of the entrées to indicate what kind of mystery meat was swimming in the grease. They certainly needed the signs. You couldn't tell from looking at the food, and you probably wouldn't be able to tell by the flavor, either.

He grabbed a tray off the top of the stack and felt some kind of food residue stick to his fingers, so he tossed the dirty tray aside and picked up another. It was even dirtier. After several attempts, he finally found one that was still wet from the dishwasher, but at least it was clean. He pushed his tray along the stainless-steel rails and scanned the menu as the line progressed toward the grill.

In front of him three sailors and a Marine good-naturedly pushed and shoved one another. Just ahead of them, at the head of the line, stood an old man of about seventy in black-rimmed glasses and wearing a gray suit and hat ten years out of fashion. The cashier had just finished ringing up his order. "Two-fifty," she told him in that flat, emotionless voice that people get when they work from midnight till seven in the morning.

The old man turned and pointed at the string of military men behind him. "Ring theirs up, too. I'm buying their breakfast. Whatever they want, it's on me." His voice rang with patriotic sentiment.

The Marine and the three sailors were all smiles as they each took turns thanking the good Samaritan. Dirty Shirt felt a surge of pride. Obviously the old man was making a statement. He was probably aware of how it felt to be in the military while protestors went on and on about the war and considered any man in uniform to be scum.

Dirty Shirt figured the old man's kindness had gotten to him because he was tired from the long flight, the funeral, the old lady and the hippies who had hassled him. He considered ordering a big breakfast, then muttered to himself, "Willy Nickel," and contented himself with coffee and a sweet roll. After all, he figured, the man's gesture was the important thing; the meal itself wasn't.

Dirty Shirt found a table to himself. He took a sip of coffee, burning the roof of his mouth, then took a bite of the roll. Chewing slowly, he recalled how he had felt when he volunteered for the Special Forces. He was certain that once he had won his beret every woman in the free world would melt at his feet. Dirty Shirt shook his head sadly. Wrong. Instead of favorably impressing women, a Green Beret disgusted them or made them very afraid. It was bad enough being a GI with short hair, but a baby-killing SFer was the worse. Dirty Shirt decided he had grown accustomed to such prejudice but would never grow used to its existence.

He heard footsteps and turned to see the old man poised beside him with a big smile on his face. "Mind if I join you?" the man asked.

"No, go ahead." He made room on the table.

The old man put down his tray and sat opposite Dirty Shirt. Stirring his coffee with his thumb, he said, "All the other military men decided to live it up at my expense. Bacon, eggs, hash browns and toast. Of course I knew they would. They always do. But you're different. From the size of you I know you don't eat like a bird, but you only took a Danish and coffee. Why?"

Dirty Shirt took a sip of coffee. It had cooled some. "Willy Nickel, that's why."

"Go on."

"Willy and me were shoeshine boys. I grew up dirt-poor. In fact, that's where I got my nickname—Dirty Shirt. Hard to keep clean when you're blacking soles and shining shoes. Anyway, my partner's nickname was Willy Nickel. We all thought he was a little slow because whenever he was done shining shoes, the grown men would pay him for the shine, then would hold out a handful of change and let Willy choose his tip. He always took a nickel. Never a dime or quarter.

"The men would hoot and holler at his stupidity because Willy could have just as easily taken dimes or quarters. They were so flabbergasted that they'd do it again and again, telling him, 'Go on, Willy, take whatever you want out of my hand.' And Willy always took a nickel. Then they'd call over their buddies and do it some more. 'Here watch this,' they'd say. 'I told the kid he could take whatever he wanted and he only took a nickel. You try it with him and you'll see.'"

By now the old man was leaning forward and grinning.

Dirty Shirt continued. "So one day I pulled Willy aside and told him he was dumb and that he should take the quarter next time it was offered. Willy laughed. Told me the first time he took the quarter was the last time they played the game. That's when he told me how much he was bringing home in tips. By then it was too late for me to start playing dumb, or I would have. I've thought about it a lot since then. And you know, he was right."

"Willy Nickel. Interesting story," said the old man. "I can see myself right there at the shoeshine stand feeding Willy nickel after nickel and never once figuring out his scam. What happened to him?"

"I buried him yesterday at Arlington National Cemetery."

After that Dirty Shirt went over and got refills of coffee and the two of them talked about how the old man had been a B-29 pilot in World War II, shot down twice, and how his daughter and her unborn baby had been killed the year before by a drunk driver. And how he was a retired lawyer in Washington and came out to the airport every morning before going to the office.

They talked some more and then the old man left and Dirty Shirt wandered out into the concourse where all the molded plastic chairs were bolted to the floor so that no one could steal them. He wondered what fool thought anyone would ever want to.

After searching up and down the length of the concourse, Dirty Shirt finally picked out a spot where no one was sitting. Shortly afterward, the sailors he had seen in the cafeteria line came over and sat down one row behind him. A moment later he felt someone else plop down right next to him. He turned to see what his companion looked like. But he was sorry when he looked at her.

Garbed in a huge black overcoat, the woman appeared to be in her thirties, weighing about three hundred pounds. With her black hair dyed a cheap red, and deep purple circles under her eyes, she looked like a woman on her last legs. Looking directly at the Green Beret sergeant, she smiled.

Dirty Shirt figured it best not to encourage small talk, so he faced forward, hoping she'd get the message. No such luck.

"You're in the Army, huh?" she said in a high-pitched voice that grated on his nerves. It sure wasn't his day, Dirty Shirt thought ruefully. First the old blue-haired dragon, and now this.

He nodded. He didn't have to talk to her, but he didn't have to be rude, either, he decided.

She gave him a conspiratorial wink. "You know, I'm not wearing any clothes under my coat."

"How nice for you," Shirt muttered.

"In fact, I'm stark naked."

Dirty Shirt closed his eyes and groaned. "Oh, Lord, why me?" In an attempt at self-defense, he looked her squarely in the eye, put on his war face and hoped the ploy would scare her off.

Instead she unbuttoned the top button on her coat and gave a little shrug of her shoulders, opening the coat a little wider and exposing an ample amount of pink flesh. "You know, men pay good money to spend time with me. You'll never guess what I do for a living."

"You're a college girl. No, wait, a lawyer's wife."

She batted her eyelashes. "No, silly. I'm a prostitute."

"Never would have guessed."

She looked at him coyly. "You know, you're kind of handsome, in a rugged way. Would you like to spend some time with me in a more intimate surrounding? We could catch a cab somewhere."

"Yeah, I'd probably catch God knows what else, too," he mumbled.

"I usually charge a hundred dollars an hour," she said in her scratchy voice. "But for a guy like you, I'd do it for nothing. You turn me on. Come on. I'll sneak into one of the stalls in the men's room with you. It'll only take a minute."

Dirty Shirt twisted his beret back and forth in his hands. "Boy, I'd like to. I really would. But I'm a happily married man and I take my vows very seriously."

"Oh, that's sweet. What's her name?"

"Oh, uh, Margie."

She looked at him incredulously. "Well, you silly goose, Margie will never know unless you tell her. She'd probably get all jealous and upset. And you wouldn't do that. You wouldn't want to hurt her, if you love her."

Sighing, he responded, "Yeah. But I'd know, deep inside. And I could never live with the shame. If I made love to you, I'd have to shoot myself afterward."

"Aw, come on, you're just shy." She reached inside her purse and pulled out a half-pint bottle of peppermint schnapps and pushed it toward him. "You just need a couple of drinks to loosen you up. Drink up. A slug of this will get the juices flowing."

He could see the schnapps was half-empty. He shuddered. The thought of sipping from a bottle her lips had touched revolted him. "Lady, there's not enough whiskey in the world."

"I see," she said, somewhat miffed. "Okay. If you're religious, a Jesus freak or something, I understand." She nodded, got up and waddled over to where the three sailors were sitting.

Dirty Shirt watched as she plopped down next to them. The sailors broke off their conversation long enough to stare at the apparition and then went back into their huddle, ignoring her. Frowning, she smacked one of them hard on the shoulder, almost knocking him out of the chair. When he looked up to glare at her, she smiled and said, "So, you're in the Navy, huh? Guess what I'm wearing underneath this coat...."

Dirty Shirt shook his head and muttered, "No, ma'am, there's not enough whiskey in the world."

14

NVA BASE CAMP
CAMBODIA

Somewhat depressed by the ambush of the American soldiers, Morrow and Maxwell were silent on the trail. Night had fallen by the time Dinh's unit had quick-marched to the outskirts of the enemy camp. From the jungle twenty or thirty yards out, Maxwell could see the glow from the bamboo-kindled cookfires. The flickering flames caused the shadows of the trees to dance as if in some macabre ritual.

Once they reached the clearing and trooped in among the huts, the villagers who had been left behind started anxiously asking the raiding party who had been killed and wounded.

One tearful woman, her face contorted in anguish, hung on Dinh's shirt as he spoke to her. When he fell silent, her knees weakened and she started to collapse, threatening to drag him to the ground with her. Dinh had just told her that her husband had been killed in the fighting. Finally two other women came up to the bereaved wife and dragged her away, the other two doubtlessly feeling superior because their men had done battle with the Americans without having to sacrifice their own lives for the cause.

The soldiers pushed through the crowd and during the next hour cleaned their weapons and stored their gear. This impressed the CIA man. The simple fact that they cleaned their weapons, thereby taking care of business first, marked them as a disciplined fighting force and not a ragtag pack of weekend warriors. It meant they were to be taken seriously as a foe. Maxwell found himself respecting them.

He noticed that the soldiers who had taken part in the raid were showered with attention, while the men who had stayed behind stood off in a small group by themselves and were ignored, their facial expressions varying from shame to anger. When they had first entered the village, Maxwell had noticed an attractive young woman in a white blouse and black skirt who had been standing face-to-face with a man, the two of them holding hands. But now she sat next to one of the raiders, and her previous partner stood alone by his hut, looking sullen and rejected.

Morrow had noticed the subtle attitudes. "Something is going on that I don't understand," said Morrow. "I wish I had taken a course in anthropology back in college. I wish I knew a little about these people's mores and social customs. Seems there's some kind of rift between the village women and their husbands. They're throwing themselves at Dinh's men. I don't think they're afraid or feel it's something they have to do. I'm sure they want it this way. I don't understand it. Jerry, do you know anything about these people's customs?"

Maxwell shrugged noncommittally. "I don't know. Things probably haven't changed out here in ten thousand years. I'd say all this has to do with the fact that basically there are two kinds of men in the world."

Morrow detected a twinge of cynicism in his voice. "What are you talking about?" she asked warily.

He grinned. "It's like this. A woman can tell a man she wants him to father her children, or she can tell him she wants him to be her children's father. One way it's a compliment. The other is roughly akin to a very long stretch in a federal penitentiary where you're required to say 'Yes, dear, whatever you want, dear' on a daily basis."

"So what's Jerry Maxwell's enlightened philosophy got to do with Dinh and his band of merry men?"

"The campfire mentality," he said. "Throwback to the Stone Age. Out of necessity, the women and the weaker males hang around the campfire. The hunter-warriors come and go. But while they're out on the prowl, the mothers and children rely on the weaker males. They need them to survive, which sets up an interesting set of circumstances. You see, the campfire women hate the weaker males because they're not strong and aggressive like the hunter-warrior types. Still, they *are* stronger than the females and therefore indispensable for minor chores and some measure of protection.

"To keep these guys compliant, the women spread their legs every now and then. Ah, but when the stronger male comes marching back to the campfire with blood on his hands and a slain buck draped over his shoulder, pussy-whipped Charlie is left out in the cold and warrior man warms his bones next to the woman. He has her whenever and wherever he wants her. And she loves it."

By now Maxwell and Morrow had started a cookfire and were staring into the flames. The glow made Morrow's face seem more beautiful as she spoke. "Yes, the highly esteemed hunter-warrior theory. I've heard it before. And I'll concede that you're at least partly correct, but your logic is a bit simplistic."

"How so?"

"I've noticed it with Mack. When he's been in a firefight, his adrenaline is all pumped up. You can feel it. You get a vicarious thrill from his experiences."

"You may have something there. Maybe that's why our culture watches war movies and reads murder mysteries."

"And why we go to amusement parks to scare the hell out of ourselves with roller coasters and the like."

"It's safer than walking point."

Morrow tossed a pebble into the fire, knocking a chunk of bamboo deeper into the glowing red coals. Searching the embers, she imagined she could see her face as she would look when she was an old woman. She was pleased with what she saw.

"Hey, not to change the subject by too many klicks, know what the definition of an expert is, Jerry?"

"No. I'll bite. What?"

"Somebody from at least a hundred miles away who has a slide show. Yeah, for once I agree with you. Our society almost looks with disgust on the married man who tries to get a little strange stuff, while the rover, the rake, the lady's man is worshiped. Our literature is peppered with tales of cuckolded husbands."

The two of them sat in silence, watching a wiry Vietnamese woman massaging a soldier's neck and back. After a while he looked over his shoulder at her and barked something unintelligible. A moment later the two of them headed off towards a clump of bushes, the woman smiling proudly, the man strutting like a rooster as darkness enveloped them.

"Hell, under the skin, more accurately between the ears, these people are no different than we are. We just have fancier toys with more buttons and fancy geegaws to do our heavy lifting for us. But the essence of man, the genetic memory handed down through the millenium, is a carbon copy. Maybe they're a little more open about the sex thing than we are.''

"You want me to narrow down the concept for you, Jerry? It's called survival of the fittest. You do what you've got to do to stay alive.''

"Yeah," said Maxwell. "You do what you got to do. Hey, what do you think of Dinh's rock-throwing exercise? Impressive as hell, huh?''

Morrow wondered if the display had been more for her benefit or the troops. She knew most of them weren't green, but were experienced veterans. Not that it mattered; it would still make good copy, if she could ever get out of this god-forsaken jungle. She considered whether or not it would be wise to mention her desire to leave to Dinh. Swallowing a mouthful of rice, she began to think of the amenities of civilization that she was missing.

With the heat and humidity cloaked around her, she remembered the frigid air-conditioned space inside MACV HQ. She understood what Gerber was talking about when he told her in the jungle he missed the simple luxury of tables and chairs. Morrow found herself wishing she had a simple sleeping bag.

"Chocolate bars," said Morrow wistfully. "Chocolate bars are what I miss the most." Sensually she ran the tip of her tongue around her lips.

Maxwell studied the woman's face, her glistening lips, her high cheekbones accentuated by smudges of dirt and by the light of the campfire. Her brown, almost blond hair was damp with sweat and clinging to her brow. He shuddered, feeling himself grow erect against the inside of his thigh. Then he looked away, and the two of them sat silently for a while staring into the fire, virtually ignored by the Vietnamese soldiers. The two Americans just sat there watching the fire, the logs crackling as the flames consumed them.

Maxwell had been twisting a stick in his hands, holding it like a riding crop, but with a sudden flurry of anger he hurled it into the heart of the fire. A shower of sparks fountained up from the flames. Maxwell began to talk, but his voice had taken on a curious tone, as if he were alone and talking only to himself.

"When I was a kid we got lots of Hershey bars. We were spoiled on them. But these weren't brown like the ones all the other kids packed in their lunches. When you unwrapped them, ours were covered with glaze, a frosty white glaze." He shrugged and then went on with his story. "They didn't taste any different. They only looked different. I never knew why that was until a couple of years ago when I asked my old man about it. He turned red and his voice cracked when he told me those were the only ones he could afford for his kids.

"You see, Dad worked as a janitor for a vending machine company and they gave him a deal on the bars that were so old they had whitened. Still perfectly safe to eat, but that funny white color didn't make a favorable impression on the customers who had paid a nickel for a candy bar. So they dumped them at a big loss and my old man took advantage of it. To this day I hate chocolate."

Morrow caught the significance of what he had just told her. "Oh, I don't know. I mean, with your Ivy League background, I just naturally assumed you had money. I didn't know."

Maxwell stared intently at the fire, as if ashamed to meet her gaze. "Yeah. Jerry Maxwell. Blueblood. We were dirt-poor, Robin. I've had to fight and connive my whole life. I had to work my way through Yale as a short-order cook in a stainless-steel diner." He had put special emphasis on the word *work*.

Tenderly Robin touched his shoulder. He turned his head and gazed into her eyes.

His voice took on an ominous tone. "Robin, you realize we may not survive this one. After all we've seen, they can never let us go." He paused to let the seriousness of their situation sink in. "We might die right here in this stinking jungle. They probably won't even find our bones."

"I know, Jerry. I know," she reassured him. She had already faced that possibility during their first few days of captivity and had come to terms with it.

He shifted closer until they were touching and he was close enough to wrap his arm around her shoulder. "Robin," he murmured, "I know we've had our differences over the past couple of months, but in spite of all that I'm asking you to forget my past and maybe give me a chance, and I'd rest easy in my lonely—"

"Whatever's on your mind, Jerry, just say it. Don't beat around the bush."

"Okay." He gave an exaggerated sigh. "I sure could use a hug about now. Do you think you could . . . ?"

She smiled, wrapped her arms around him and gave him a motherly hug. She patted him on the back as if that would somehow make everything work out in the end, that they would come out of their predicament alive. She hoped she was right.

Her warm breath touched the side of his neck. Pressed light against him, her breasts heaved with each breath that she took. He went on, "I've been a fool, Robin. Working so hard to be a success, trying to be everything my father wasn't. I guess I've missed out on the important things in life."

"Like friendship," said Morrow.

He sighed as if he were unloading decades worth of anguish. "Yes, Robin. Things like friendship." He paused for a moment before going on. "And intimacy."

There was a dead silence. Robin had an idea where he was going.

He pulled away, and before she could react he had cupped her face in his hands and kissed her full on the lips. He could tell from the look in her green eyes that the move had startled her. She pulled back with a look of confusion, but he had expected that. He struck quickly, hoping to keep her off guard. "Robin, I want to make love to you."

Her eyes widened. "What?" she said incredulously.

"We may be killed. No, we will be killed, and I can't stand the thought of dying in this godforsaken land. Robin, let me make love to you."

She pushed him away and stood up. Arms folded across her chest, she turned her back on him. "Don't be ridiculous," she said.

He scrambled to his feet and scurried around to meet her gaze. "Please, Robin," he purred. "You know you want to. If we're going to go out, let's go out with at least a little pleasure. Mack needn't know. I promise."

She looked at him with disgust. "You want a sympathy fuck, huh? You've actually got the nerve to ask for a sympathy fuck? Well, at least you didn't whine, whimper and beg. Or is that your idea of foreplay, Jerry? Is that what's next on the agenda?"

His face reddened. "Only if it turns you on, Robin."

15

AN AMERICAN OUTPOST SOMEWHERE IN THE JUNGLE

Master Sergeant Anthony B. Fetterman was standing next to Lieutenant Carrington in the chow line that wound outside and around the tent when someone behind them yelled, "Ten-hut," followed by the terse reply, "As you were."

Without bothering to turn around, Carrington muttered, "That will be Colonel Staley. He's one tough son of a bitch. You've heard the description, command presence, well, he typifies it. Back in World War II he started out a buckass private in the infantry, won a bunch of Silver Stars and rose through the ranks. The ringknockers in this division hate his fucking guts because he still acts like an enlisted man. They may hate him for it, but they also respect him for his leadership abilities."

Fetterman glanced at Carrington's hand, interested to note whether or not the young lieutenant wore a class ring that would indicate he was a West Point graduate. The finger was as bare as a bone, meaning both he and Colonel Staley qualified as ducks out of water with the USMA ringknockers.

Gerber had told Fetterman all about it, how in staff meetings when OCS officers said something the West Point graduates didn't like, they would immediately start rapping their class rings on the tabletop, drowning out the OCS guy. Without the benefit of their own class ring, the OCS officers were mute.

The colonel walked right past the two of them and addressed Fetterman over his shoulder. "Where's your brain bucket, son?"

Fetterman bristled. Even though they looked to be the same age, he had called Fetterman "son."

The colonel did a double take. Then, as if he were seeing the master sergeant for the first time, Staley took a step back. "Whoa, wait a minute," he corrected himself. "Sorry, Master Sergeant. Sometimes us old war horses can't see the forest for the trees. I'm so used to seeing eighteen-year-old airheads running around without their head gear that I automatically assumed you were one of them. No offense intended."

Sergeant Fetterman sized the colonel up by his own personal yardstick, immediately noticing the subdued combat infantryman's badge and jump wings. Instead of wearing fatigues with enough starch to stand up on their own, the colonel's were merely clean and pressed, which was a much more sensible approach. Without being smothered in starch, they would wear cooler and hang more comfortably on his lean frame, though they wouldn't look as sharp.

The colonel's boots were polished but not spit-shined. And instead of a pearl-handled revolver and a western-style gunfighter's belt thick with cartridges like some hot dog fieldgrade officer, Staley carried a U.S. Army-issue .45-caliber automatic in a plain black holster on his web belt along with a bayonet. Fetterman decided he liked him fine and would go on patrol with him anytime. The master sergeant took a second glance at the bayonet; it, too, was untraditional.

The colonel noticed Fetterman's obvious scrutiny. He grinned broadly, showing a set of perfect teeth. "Ya like it, huh? Real conversation piece."

The parkerized bayonet rasped as he pulled the well-honed blade from its scabbard. Blade first, he handed it to Fetterman, who recognized it as an M-1 carbine bayonet. But instead of sporting the conventional brown leather grip, it was fitted with crystal-clear Plexiglas, fitted to conform perfectly to his own hand.

Fetterman carefully stroked his thumb across the edge—it was razor-sharp. He didn't doubt for a moment that the colonel had honed it that way himself, unlike others in power who would have delegated the job to an aide.

"I ended up stationed in Okinawa after Hiroshima and Nagasaki," explained the colonel. "Our property disposal units were stuck with surplus B-29s, trucks and jeeps. They didn't know what to do with them, so they dumped 'em over the cliffs to get rid of them. What a god-awful waste of war material. And just a couple of years later we could have used it all in Korea." He shook his head in disgust before going on. "Anyway, me and some buddies climbed down the rocks, nearly breaking our necks in the process, and yanked out a section of Plexiglas windshield from a bomber, melted it down and fitted it to our bayonets."

Fetterman had also served during World War II. "I saw action in Europe," the Special Forces sergeant said. He thought he'd politely give the colonel an opportunity to ask for details.

The colonel grunted in reply. He ignored Fetterman and went on with his chest-thumping. "I served under General Joe Stilwell. Trained for jungle warfare in India. I was one of the original Merrill's Marauders in northern Burma. Kicked the Japs' asses at Walawbum. And Okinawa. Also fought the chinks in Korea. Spent all my life killing Orientals. Don't like 'em much. Make no secret of it.'' He swung around and pointed toward the jungle, sweeping his arm in a wide arc. "Somewhere out there lurks a host of enemy soldiers. And with a hundred good men, hand-picked fire-pissers, men like you and me, we could march through the whole NVA."

By now they had worked their way through the chow line and were seated at a table eating bacon and eggs. Snowflake had winked at Fetterman and served him a double portion of bacon. And they were talking about how the war was being mismanaged by civilians. Fetterman voiced his opinion. "Maybe they'll finally get it together. I expect this latest Tet offensive got their attention all up and down the halls of the Pentagon."

The colonel guffawed. "We went through the same thing a hundred years ago. Washington wouldn't let the Army fight the Indian War. The Sioux braves were winning until the cavalry started to use guerrilla tactics and didn't allow the Indians to retreat in winter. When the politics in Washington let the cavalry start pressing the Sioux during the winter, they were no longer able to rebuild as they had in previous years. The Army kept the pressure up and transformed the war from the way the Sioux wanted to fight it to the way the Army wanted to fight it."

Fetterman used his fork to push his bacon aside. "You're right. Nothing's changed in a hundred years. Today in Vietnam it's the same way. If Victor Charlie wants to come out into the open and fight, we oblige him. If he retreats, we retreat as well."

Staley picked up a strip of bacon from his own plate, took a bite and muttered, "I don't blame you. This bacon is too damn salty again this morning."

Carrington added his opinion on the Vietnam War. "There are other similarities to consider," he said. "Like the forts in the old West, the ones the cavalry troopers used as bases to chase Indians. The Apaches always knew where they were. This outpost we're constructing won't be any different. It wasn't until the cavalry began to make Indian-style hit-and-run raids, living off the land and chasing the savages wherever they tried to run, that the Army was able to fight effectively."

Staley was working on another strip of bacon. Between bites he interjected, "It's the same in Vietnam. Most places the night belongs to Charlie. And if he's not fighting and dying, the U.S. troops don't actively look for him. If he's chased out of an operational area, he's chased not much beyond the proximity. Often an area belongs outright to the VC."

Fetterman nodded. "A Shau Valley."

Staley added, "Probably happen up yonder at Khe Sanh, too, once the siege ends. The Marines will leave and Charlie will move right in. Fuck the goddamn jarheads anyhow. They deserve whatever they get, still hanging on to the old M-14."

Fetterman asked him what he had against the M-14.

"What?" the colonel snapped.

Fetterman changed his tack. "I notice you're hard of hearing."

"Well, you're a ballsy son of a bitch, aren't you, Sergeant?"

Fetterman grinned, then shrugged. "I got something on my mind, I spit it out. Figure dancing around the issue is a waste of time and an insult to a thinking man."

"Works for me. And you're right, I've got partial hearing loss, upper frequency level, I don't have to tell you it's an occupational hazard with all the loud noises in a combat zone.''

Fetterman added, ''That and the whining and whimpering of the Saigon commandos.''

Colonel Staley snickered and continued talking about his hearing loss. ''And they can't give you a Purple Heart for it. Just the same, there ought to be some kind of award or commendation. The royal order of the ruptured eardrum, with the deaf son of a bitch cluster. Long as you've been in, I figure you've got a touch of it, too. Am I right?''

Fetterman nodded. ''Omaha Beach, first day. Kraut tracer rounds cracking overhead, 88s exploding all around my nose. I'm just happy I didn't lose more than my hearing.''

The colonel shifted his weight from one buttock to the other and began poking at his eggs. ''I've been able to compensate through the years by listening real careful and assuming nothing. It's funny. It's more natural to only half pay attention to what the other guy has to say. But guys like you and me, we have to work hard to keep up. I figure that gives us an edge over the old soldiers with good hearing who have trouble keeping awake during a briefing.''

Suddenly Lieutenant Carrington blurted out, ''Why didn't you old guys wear earplugs or something?''

Fetterman just stared at the kid for a moment. ''Old guys,'' he said. ''Did he call us old guys?''

The colonel's eyes sparkled as he looked on. He either hadn't heard what had been said or was amused instead of offended by it.

Fetterman looked at Carrington as if he was crazy, then shrugged it off. ''On patrol you need all your senses, especially your ears, so you don't go wandering around with 'em plugged up. And once you're in a firefight, there isn't time to stop shooting long enough to unscrew the little carrying case and stick 'em in. And, quite frankly, Charlie doesn't care if you lose your hearing.''

Fetterman unholstered his .45-caliber automatic and dropped the clip into the palm of his hand. With the pistol lying across his lap, he shucked two rounds out of the magazine and stuck one in each of his ears.

"Here's a little trick I learned from the Aussies. You look stupid, but what the hell, they make good earplugs.''

The colonel borrowed a cigarette from the next table over, tore off the filter and held it out for the lieutenant to see. "Mosquitoes bother you at night, you can also use these to keep 'em from driving you crazy. Of course if you do that, you may not hear the zip who walks up to you and sticks his bayonet into your belly. So you see, son, what you're trading is your sense of hearing later in life in order to survive.''

After breakfast came word on the radio that Nha Trang would send a Huey for Fetterman in three days. In the meantime he would be stranded at FSB Rio Indio. Colonel Staley asked Fetterman whether or not he had had much experience setting up camp defenses. When Fetterman modestly indicated he had some, the three of them took a tour of the fire support base, which was code-named Rio Indio. Fetterman and the colonel talked as they walked, with Lieutenant Carrington silently tagging along beside them.

"Do you speak Vietnamese, Sergeant Fetterman?'' asked the colonel. Without even waiting for an answer he went on to say, "Sweet Jesus, the good Lord knows I've tried to learn it out of a book and dutifully listening to the Defense Language Institute's tapes in my billet at night. But I'll be damned if this zip lingo doesn't sound like two cats mating out in the alley.'' He stopped and turned to look squarely at Fetterman. "Worst thing, the worst fucking thing, and I don't know if you know it or not, son. . . .'' He paused as if waiting for Fetterman to tell him it was okay to spring this forbidden knowledge on him.

"What's that, Colonel?"

"I know you've seen a lot, son, living up in the hills with those savages, running those little hit-and-run raids. Of course I suspect you guys do more running than hitting." He chuckled at his own joke before pausing to bite his lip. Then with an air of great seriousness he continued. "Did you know these people eat dogs? Did you know they cook their fucking dogs?"

Fetterman remembered the Montagnard tribesman and the meal he had shared with them. "I've heard that."

The colonel shook his head in disgust. "Knowing they'd do such a thing makes one wonder if they don't drag off their dead because they're also goddamn cannibals. Considering some of the things they do to our boys, it wouldn't surprise me in the least. Bad as they are, they're still better than the goddamn Koreans, though. Those crazy ROK sons of bitches bury cabbage in the ground and let it rot for a couple of months before they dig it up and eat it. Ever smell a Korean's breath, Sergeant?"

The colonel stopped dead in his tracks and whirled to his left. Apparently he had seen something out of the corner of his eye. "Is that it? Did it finally get here?" he said inquisitively, poking a stubby finger at a deuce-and-a-half with a strange profile squatting smack in the center of its cargo bed. The tarpaulin and bows that usually covered the back had been removed and some sort of weapons system had been mounted on its bed. Oblivious of the group, an enlisted man was standing behind the weapon, staring into its sights.

Carrington mumbled with little enthusiasm that the big truck had rumbled in after he had already retired for the evening.

Staley told Fetterman the weapon was his pride and joy. "Somebody in Saigon dreamed it up, mounting a Browning M-2 fifty-caliber machine gun on a mobile platform and figuring it would be good for perimeter work. We've never had a chance to use it yet, so I made sure we got one for Rio Indio. It's never seen the elephant, but we'll change that right quick." The colonel trotted over for a closer look.

Standing alongside the truck, Fetterman studied the creation with awe. He'd heard stories about these things but had never actually seen one before. Mounted on the flatbed of a two-and-a-half ton truck, an ordnance man had adjusted the headspace of the bolt so that it would fire one shot at a time instead of the long, slow bursts of a conventional M-2. A range-finding scope had been fitted to the fifty cal and had been zeroed in at five thousand yards. It was, in essence, a sniper rifle capable of shooting down a MiG fighter. The fact that it fired a bullet as big as your thumb was overkill, Fetterman conceded, but the key to its effectiveness would be its ungodly range, nearly four times that of a conventional .30-caliber sniper rifle. With memories of the number of times he had seen A-camps overrun, Fetterman decided to at least provisionally approve of the awesome creation, no matter what the Geneva Convention lawmakers in three-piece suits thought.

Standing next to the truck and looking up at his pride and joy, the colonel rubbed his hands with unconcealed glee. "Think it will matter if I crank off a shot or two?"

"Of course not," said Lieutenant Carrington, mindful of the fact that only generals say no to colonels. He didn't want to end up at a duty station in Greenland.

With the practiced moves of a man who had done it a thousand times before, the colonel hooked his boot in the metal stirrup welded to the tailgate, gracefully swung up onto the bed of the deuce-and-a-half and padded forward toward the gun.

As Staley fawned over the receiver, the gunsight and the cocking handle, Fetterman noticed a sparkle in his eye and a spring in his step that hadn't been there a moment ago when they had been merely touring the compound. Funny what a new toy will do for a man's attitude, he mused.

Colonel Staley pulled off his steel helmet and lobbed it at the Special Forces sergeant, who caught it and promptly placed it on his own bare head. No one said anything; no one had even noticed.

With both hands grasping the butterfly trigger, Staley stuck his nose alongside the gun and peered through the optical sight. "This weapon locked and loaded, Lieutenant Carrington?" he asked sternly.

Carrington looked at the sergeant who had been manning the gun. The man nodded. "Yes, Colonel," responded Carrington.

"Then stand clear. I intend to warm up the barrel with a couple of rounds." The colonel's demeanor had taken on a more serious edge. The armorer stepped away, leaned back against the cab of the truck and crossed his arms.

The colonel's mouth cracked a cruel grin. He stepped to the left and then to the right, swinging the barrel of the gun in a narrow arc as he searched downrange for a target of opportunity. "I see a clearing," he said to no one in particular.

The armorer nodded. He had been staring at it for fifteen minutes before the brass arrived. He knew the bald patch of ground well enough to draw a picture of it. Dead center were the errant gusts of wind that stirred up the red dust, creating whirling eddies. The deep greens of the ankle-high grass stopped suddenly at the tree line where sky-high teak, balsa and other nameless vegetation crowded closely together. But while the sergeant knew the clearing well, he hadn't seen anything move there other than the plant life swaying in the wind.

Intent on firing the weapon, the colonel used the markings etched into the lens to calculate the distance from the truck to the clearing. He estimated the range at just over four thousand yards.

"Hold it," he said, again to no one in particular. "I see movement in the grass." He knew not to look for contrast when searching for a target, because even a halfway decent camouflage job could hide what you wanted to see. Instead, he looked for detectable motion.

When he finally saw something, he started to babble excitedly. "A zip. Fucking Commie, NVA. Goddamn stupid dog-eating fools."

Carrington's expression and tone of voice betrayed concern. "Colonel, he could be alone or he could be a point man for a company or even a battalion. Maybe we should send out a patrol."

The colonel looked away from the gunsight and stared incredulously at the lieutenant. After a moment he responded in a mocking voice. "No, shit. Ya really think so?" Then he went back to the gun, looking intently into the lens and alternately smacking the side and bottom of the sighting mechanism to make minute adjustments in his point of aim. "Looks like I've got a clear shot," he said quietly.

He held his breath and stood motionless. After a few moments, he pressed the butterfly trigger and the gun roared, rocking the truck on its springs and flipping the driver's door open.

A moment later the colonel was still peering intently down the sights. "Bullet ought to be getting there right about now," he said. Then he jumped away from the gun, whooping and hollering. "Got that motherfucker right between the numbers."

Fetterman climbed up onto the truck and peeked through the gunsights. He could see a man down on the ground, sprawled flat on his back with his arms flung out to either side. A moment later a second NVA soldier ran out from the trees, his face a blend of puzzlement and grief as he knelt beside his fallen comrade. A wide blotch of red was spreading on the dead man's chest where the big slug had caught him.

Fetterman knew the exit wound would be larger and had probably torn out the spine and half of the internal organs. Then five more VC came running out of the brush and crouched around the dead man. They held a hurried conference, pointing in the direction of the American compound. Finally they slipped back into the tree line, dragging their fallen comrade by his wrists.

The colonel playfully nudged Fetterman. "Better than hunting deer. And you don't have to clean the sons of bitches."

Before he could answer, they heard the ominous thunk of a mortar firing. They had little time to seek cover before the exploding shells rained down upon them.

"Incoming!" someone yelled.

Fetterman and Staley jumped off the back of the truck and started running side by side, heading for cover, which happened to be the roofless stone house. The master sergeant shouted, "Looks like you stirred up a nest of hornets!"

The colonel answered, "That's my job, sonny."

THE WALLS OF THE HOUSE measured a foot and a half thick, and even with the roof already blown off and the insides of the structure charred black, Fetterman found consolation in the fact that the only thing that could knock it out was a direct hit.

The enemy soldiers had only fired a token salvo of six mortar rounds. It had been quiet for more than an hour. Head elevated barely above the windowsill, Fetterman peered through binoculars at the tree line, searching for signs of enemy activity. Unfortunately he couldn't see much detail, the visibility impaired by morning haze. Fortunately the sun would burn it off by midmorning.

An unshaven soldier with dark circles under his eyes brought the colonel a canteen cup full of black coffee. The colonel tore open a sugar packet and poured it into the metal container.

"Who's going to split this coffee with me?" he asked. Although the question was phrased as an open invitation, Staley looked squarely at the PFC who had brought him the cup. "You'll split this with me, won't you, son?" asked the old man.

"Yes, sir," said the PFC.

The colonel lifted his cup to his lips. "To tomorrow," he said.

"Yes, Colonel, to tomorrow."

Staley was ignoring everyone but the PFC. "Hell of a way to serve the Lord's calling, being a damn enlisted man. I was a private once. Worked my way up through the ranks." His brow furrowed; he seemed deep in thought. "And I never forgot where I came from. Goddamn politicians. Goddamn management techniques. They're going to ruin this damn war for us. You don't run a war like you do a corporation. We need leaders, not pansy-fucking MBAs." The colonel good-naturedly slapped the PFC on the back as if they were hunting buddies waiting to kill ducks at dawn. "How 'bout you, son? What did you do before the war?"

"I was a drummer, Colonel. In a rock and roll band."

"A drummer, huh? In a rock and roll band?" said the colonel. "Well, at least you're not a goddamn MBA ring-knocker."

Fetterman picked up the binoculars and scanned the tree line. Things were a little too quiet, he thought.

"They're going to try to overrun us, aren't they?" asked Carrington with some concern.

"What do you think?" Fetterman said curtly. It was a statement, not a question.

"I feel like a virgin," said Carrington with dead seriousness. "I know what's going to happen, but I don't know how it's going to feel."

Fetterman nodded. "So you've never been under fire before, and when it finally happens, you're afraid you'll be afraid."

"Or worse."

"What's worse?"

"Running."

Fetterman understood. "Where would you run to?"

"I don't know. You know what I mean."

Fetterman's voice took on a fatherly tone. "Yeah, I know. Only the way I figure it, I'd be more worried about the day when you're not afraid. Because if that happens, it means you're either crazy or a fool."

"Any idea what I should do?" asked Carrington.

"There's not that much to it. The first mistake new guys make is to freeze and bunch up together for security. They drop to the ground and just lie there, pissing their pants and not firing back." Fetterman shook his head. "I saw one man just lay there while a VC came right up and shot him. A vet dives for cover, won't stay where he's exposed and fires back at a target, not into the blue."

"Tracers scare the hell out of me," said the lieutenant, shaking his head. "Taking a bullet would be bad enough, but a tracer..."

Fetterman shrugged. "Me, I like tracers. Charlie fires tracers up high and his other guns low in a grazing fire. You see the green tracers high and think you're okay, so you try to crawl, but you get a bullet in the nose for your trouble."

Carrington grimaced. "More than running, I'm scared of getting shot. Not the bullet tearing me up, or losing an arm or leg. The pain. I wonder if I can endure the pain and not cry out like some of the guys you hear about who end up crying for their mothers. Jesus, I don't want to be reduced to that."

Fetterman tapped the side of his head. "It's up here. All of it's up here." He pulled his shirt up over his back and motioned for the lieutenant to look.

Carrington gazed at the depression in Fetterman's back just below his left shoulder blade. It looked as if some of his flesh was missing and the skin had caved in.

"My God, what happened to you?"

Fetterman dropped his shirt and stared at the lieutenant. "I'll give you one guess."

"Oh, right. A bullet hole," he said, somewhat chagrined.

"That's one of the two I own. And I can tell you I'm no longer afraid of being shot. I know what it feels like. Fear is just not knowing what's going to happen or how something's going to feel."

Across the room the PRC/25 on the OD field table crackled to life. "We got activity" came the tersely worded message. At Fetterman's insistence they had sent out a reconnaissance patrol, which was now reporting in.

"It's like a beehive out here," continued the voice on the radio. The patrol reported seeing an NVA unit busy digging mortar emplacements, while enemy soldiers and stockpiles of ammunition were being deployed around the perimeter of Fire Support Base Rio Indio. Suddenly the unseen RTO blurted, "Listen, there's a bunch of zips sneaking out of the jungle and into the grass. Get ready. They're near enough to open fire on you."

"They're attacking!" the lieutenant yelled. The American troops took up their positions. The big machine guns in the sandbagged emplacements were pulled back twice to cock them. Fetterman cranked the TA-312 field phone and sent firing data to the mortar pits as the crew ripped open shell cases. Minutes ticked by. There was a tense silence.

Fetterman stared out of the shattered window. He didn't need the binoculars to know that the enemy was close. Then came the tinny shriek of bugles, and NVA in khaki uniforms streamed out of the trees and into the killzone the engineers had leveled around the camp. Fetterman waited craftily.

When the enemy crossed the clearing to within fifteen hundred feet of the wire, he yelled, "Give it to 'em." The big machine guns, the bipod-mounted M-60s, 81 mm mortars and M-16s opened up in a deafening salvo. Shrieks and yells came back from the field as the NVA began returning fire. A Chinese-made 122 mm rocket streaked out of the jungle, soaring clear over the Americans' heads and bursting in the trees behind the camp near a rice paddy.

The American mortarmen hung and dropped round after round. The initial shots went wide, then they found their range. Wave after wave of NVA soldiers poured out of the jungle and into the killing zone, seemingly oblivious to the heavy fire. In a few minutes bodies lay sprawled on the field. Fetterman could hear the wounded crying and moaning, but the NVA kept coming.

The lieutenant grinned. "Those little bastards must think we're amateurs. Mass-wave assaults might terrify the ARVN soldiers, but to GIs they're nothing but good target practice."

Fetterman corrected him. "This isn't a mass-wave assault," he said patiently. "This is a foray."

The NVA attacked in squads, probing the defensive line, stabbing here and there. The Americans just lay in their holes and blasted away. Mortar shrapnel and AK-47 bullets hummed overhead.

Fetterman looked out the window and fired three-shot bursts from his M-16. Then he saw the colonel out in the open, madly galloping toward the fifty-caliber sniper rifle mounted on the truck.

"Jesus," said Fetterman. "That crazy son of a bitch . . ."

The colonel never made it. A bullet caught him square in the chest, knocking him flat on his back out in the open. Moments later the PFC rock and roll drummer he had shared his coffee with was hovering above him. The PFC's eyes were wide with fear. In a shrill voice he recited the first-aid litany drummed into boot camp trainees at Fort Leonard Wood by drill instructors. "Stop the bleeding. Clear the airway. Protect the wound. Treat for shock."

"You're doing just fine, son," whispered the colonel. "Just keep up what you're doing." He knew he had a sucking chest wound. One bullet had penetrated the lung, and each time he breathed his lungs drew air and blood through the bullet hole and into his lungs. The colonel could see in the PFC's eyes that the man thought he was going to die.

The ex-drummer yanked the colonel's first-aid package out of the pouch clipped on his webgear. With great care he tore open the plastic wrapper, jammed it into the bullet hole and pressed the bandage over the wound, making an airtight seal. Otherwise Staley would drown in his own blood.

By this time, Fetterman had joined the PFC and the wounded colonel. The master sergeant knew that there was nothing the PFC could do to keep the older man alive. Fetterman experienced a fleeting sadness. The old soldier had survived World War II only to meet his end in this stinking hellhole of Southeast Asia.

The PFC's swearing interrupted Fetterman's thoughts. The colonel was dead.

Twenty minutes after the attack began, it abruptly halted. But Fetterman knew the NVA would try again.

16

NATIONAL AIRPORT
WASHINGTON, D.C.

They called his flight number, and Dirty Shirt got in line and waited his turn to check in. He was used to waiting, usually while chuted up and sitting alongside a C-130 Hercules at a dusty airstrip in some godforsaken country. Besides, the ticket agent seemed very efficient and the line moved right along.

When it was his turn, the pretty blond agent looked up from her station, saw the handsome man with a green beret perched at a jaunty angle on his head and reacted with a pleasant smile.

"Well, Colonel Crawley, I see there's plenty of seats in first class this morning, so we're upgrading your ticket."

Now it was Shirt's turn to smile. "That's pleasant news. It'll make the flight much more comfortable. Thank you very much. Oh, I'm not a colonel. I'm a sergeant." He pointed at his stripes.

She winked. "Oh, I know. I'm an Army brat. I call all the enlisted colonel and all the officers private. Most of them don't complain, but you should see the second lieutenants squirm. Field grade and above never say a word. Oh, and did you know drinks are free in first class?''

Dirty Shirt decided he liked this woman. All the while he had been waiting in line, she had remained a stolid figure behind the counter, ramrod and an all-business expression. But face-to-face with Dirty Shirt she had exchanged her business facade for a sweet smile that reached all the way to Georgetown. Her eyes sparkled as she leaned forward and gazed into his. ''Company policy,'' she purred. ''Empty seats in first class go to Army, as long as they're not legs,'' she added.

''Company policy?'' he repeated.

''At least when I'm assigning seats,'' she said, giggling. The two of them looked over at the wall where the standbys were waiting in hopes of making this connection. Among them were a sprinkling of backpacks and longhairs. Two of the standbys he had already met—the hippie and his chick. Inconspicuously Dirty Shirt pointed them out. ''Those two on my flight?'' he asked.

''Jesus Christ and the Virgin Mary?'' she asked.

He grinned. ''Yeah.''

''Depends. Could send them to the stable if you want.''

At that moment Dirty Shirt noticed a wide brass ring dangling on her right wrist. Then everything clicked into place. Her Montagnard bracelet was a commodity, primitive jewelry rarely seen outside of the Central Highlands, that is unless it was on the wrist of a Special Forces trooper. Of course it was always possible she had picked it up in a pawn shop. But he wanted to believe her possession of a Montagnard bracelet meant an SFer near and dear to her had given it to her.

She saw him looking at the bracelet. ''Yeah, as I was saying, it doesn't cost the airline a dime, so empty seats might as well improve your life. Oh, and did I already tell you, you'll be riding with a friend?''

He shot her a quizzical expression.

''There's another SFer already onboard.'' She touched the top of her head, meaning there was another Green Beret. ''I'll seat you next to each other so you can swap war stories and ogle the flight attendants together.''

Dirty Shirt could see she knew the character of Green Berets intimately. He pointed at her bracelet, but didn't say anything.

She placed her fingertips against it and began to twirl it on her thin wrist. ''Dad gave it to me. He's a team sergeant with the Fifth.'' Her smile was gone, and she looked terribly concerned. ''I miss him, and worry about him. Some nights I can't even sleep. I love him very much.'' She let out a big sigh, let go of the bracelet, retrieved her smile and began scribbling on the back of a scrap of paper. Finished, she pressed it into his hand. ''If you're ever in town again, we can meet for a cup of coffee or something. In the meantime you have a flight to catch.''

Or something, mused Dirty Shirt as he tucked the scrap of paper into his wallet and began to walk down the ramp and onto the plane. He breathed deeply; he could still smell her perfume. He hoped the scent would linger. The vision of her smiling face was as vivid as if he were still standing face-to-face with her. Screw the old lady with blue hair, the fat bimbo and the hippie and his chick. Things were definitely looking up.

Once on board, he made his way down the aircraft's crowded aisle until he could see the telltale green beret poking up above the seats. He nodded when he came abreast of the passenger, instinctively sensing there was something terribly out of place about the man. Then he figured it out. The beret was all wrong.

The soldier was wearing a Twelfth Group flash from an active reserve unit out of the Chicago area, and it was lined up with the middle of the man's forehead instead of directly above the left eye where it was supposed to be. And the Twelfth flash didn't match the Tenth Group paratrooper wing background pinned to his chest. A further anomaly was the way the tassles hung from the back of the beret's sweatband instead of being knotted and snipped off. All these elements added up to the fact that the man wasn't a Green Beret but a bumbling imposter.

The final nail in the coffin came when the man looked up from his magazine, saw Dirty Shirt and turned pale. Shirt thought he could hear the man gulp. Beginning to smile evilly, he took his place in the empty seat next to the imposter. Then he leaned across the seat to shake hands. "Howdy, pardner."

The man answered weakly, "Howdy." He took off his beret and folded it on his lap.

"So how's tricks?" Dirty Shirt wanted to draw the man out into the open and then cut off his legs.

The imposter shrugged stiffly, mumbling something unintelligible. Dirty Shirt guessed him to be about five-nine, but it was difficult to tell with him sitting. With sandy brown hair, he had a solid enough frame and a good strong face.

Dirty Shirt continued to size up the man. "Been noticing your beret." In one quick motion he reached across and snatched it out of the guy's hands. Holding it upside down, he studied the inside lining, noticing it was plastic, not wool, and manufactured in the U.S., not Canada. That made it PX-bought rather than issued headgear. More evidence. Dirty Shirt placed his own beret next to the copy. His lining was black woven material with stenciled letters, identifying it as beret, men's, wool, forest-green and size seven and one-eighth.

"Your costume's all wrong, *soldier*," said Dirty Shirt. He showed the imposter the knot he had tied in the headgear and told him how it was used to adjust the beret to fit the shape of an individual's head. "We soak them in hot water, put them on, then set 'em down to dry. Later we cut off the tassels. We don't let them drape down the back like a coupla loose rappeling ropes." Up to now his tone had been pleasantly conversational, but now it took on a hard edge. "You know, some of my friends would rip your beret off your head and stuff it up your ass sideways. But I won't. I should, but I won't."

The imposter's voice was surprisingly calm. "So what are you going to do? Turn me in?"

Dirty Shirt shook his head. Under normal circumstances he would have kicked the shit out of the guy and then turned him in, but here was someone who thought it grand and glorious to be in the SF, a deep and welcome contrast to the civilians he had met as of late who thought SFers were the most heathen outlaws who had ever roamed the plains.

The leg couldn't be all bad, misguided perhaps, but not without some redeeming qualities.

"No, I'm not going to embarrass you by doing that. I don't have a mean bone in my body. Besides, I figure *you* got the identity problem, not me. Why the fuck do you figure you have to go around pretending to be something you're not?"

The man didn't answer for a moment, but finally told Dirty Shirt the reason. "My girl back home dumped me for some Jody who drives a brand-new Corvette. Figured I couldn't compete with his money, so I thought maybe she'd get turned on if I came home on leave as a Green Beret."

Dirty Shirt snorted. "So did it work?"

"Yes and no. She spent time with me, bragged me up at a couple of parties. But now I'm going to be in Vietnam for a year, and I wonder what she'll be doing while I'm gone."

Dirty Shirt looked him squarely in the eye. "Sonny, you know exactly what a woman like that will be doing. She'll be at the drive-in movie in Jody's car with her legs up in the air. Believe me, you don't want to get yourself tied up with her kind.

"I've got some more advice for you. Why don't you solve this identify problem by grabbing your guts in your hands and volunteering for the Airborne School and Special Forces? Do it for yourself. Forget that woman you been hanging around with for the past thirty days."

"I don't know...."

Dirty Shirt nudged him in the ribs. "You look like you're a physical kind of guy. Most likely you could handle the PT well enough." He tapped his index finger against the other man's temple, tapping so hard he left a red mark. "Most of it's up here. If you tell yourself you can do it and refuse to quit, no matter how dark it gets, you can do it. The secret is, never give up. Once you believe that, then you can do it." He shrugged, "In fact, no one can stop you who doesn't have a loaded weapon."

Dirty Shirt flipped the beret so that it landed back on the man's lap.

"On the other hand you could keep playing with fire until the day you run into one of my meaner partners and he catches you in drag. That happens he's likely to get real upset. I might suggest you put that beret in your hope chest and not wear it again until you've earned it."

Without a word the man plucked off the jump wings and rolled them up in his PX beret.

"So what you going to do?" Shirt asked him.

"Can't say for sure."

"Just like you, I'm on my way to Nam to finish out my tour. You ever get into Nha Trang, go to the Special Forces compound and look me up. Somebody in HQ will know where I am.''

He looked confused. ''To finish your tour? I know you can't come home on leave, so why did you return to the States?''

Dirty Shirt closed his eyes for a moment, blinked, then opened them. ''Long story, Sonny. You ever show up in Nha Trang with a real green beret on your head and I'll tell you all about it.''

17

**FIREBASE RIO INDIO
SOUTH VIETNAM**

The firing died down and the surviving attackers melted into the jungle. After the deafening noise of the M-60s and M-16s, the silence was overwhelming. If it hadn't been for all the dead bodies lying on the ground beyond the perimeter, it would have been hard to believe an attack had even occurred.

Fetterman looked at Lieutenant Carrington. The Special Forces sergeant had originally wondered how the lieutenant would do in battle, partly because he had been so anxious about his first firefight. But Carrington's expression was as calm as if he had been qualifying for expert marksman at the rifle range. And he had done well.

"Sergeant Fetterman, I'm no fool. I'm charging you with the responsibility of assessing the defenses of this camp and doing whatever you need to do in order to prevent our annihilation."

Fetterman raised his eyebrows. "What about the camp's other officers?"

"They agree with me that a man of your experience should provide for our mutual defense. If that can't be done, do whatever you need to do in order to maximize the death and destruction of the attackers. We'll either get most of us out of this alive or take most of them with us.''

Fetterman just grinned. ''I got no immediate plans for dying. Why don't we compromise, Lieutenant? Let's get most of us out of this alive and kill every fucking one of the attackers and then go out and throw a drunk. After all, it's our sworn duty.''

''Agreed, so what can we expect?''

''Attacks come in threes,'' said Fetterman, remembering the attacks he had endured at the original Camp A-555. ''This was nothing more than a probe. Their strategist wanted to see where our perimeter defenses are strong and where they're weak. If they're positive they can take us out, their next attack will be intended to put us on the ropes. If they get their way, round three will be the death blow.''

Carrington gulped hard. ''Are you saying we're going to be overrun?''

Fetterman shrugged, then took a step outside and stared far across the plain of battle to the tree line where he knew Charlie was hiding. He counted the bodies of the dead attackers as best he could and considered what he knew about the camp's resources and how he had seen its men perform under fire. Then he looked Carrington straight in the eye. ''They'll attack sometime after dark. Count on it. And when they do, we'll be ready.''

Fetterman needed no further prompting, immediately assuming command, directing the soldiers to clean their weapons, open more cases of ammunition, fill and position sandbags.

''Do you know what foogas is?'' he asked Carrington.

The lieutenant shook his head.

''An expedient weapons system. You mix gasoline and oil, then set it afire in the middle of enemy troop movements.

Problem is, if we try to bury drums of it now, their snipers will pick off our men digging the holes. And they'll know where it is and avoid it."

"I don't understand. Why even bring it up?"

"Because we can still use it to good effect. We'll just modify the method of delivery."

By 1600 hours the broiling Vietnamese sun was low in the sky, glaring into the faces of the Americans as they kept their eyes focused on the field, waiting and watching for what they knew would eventually come. Two hours later dusk turned into darkness.

Carrington clicked on his flashlight to better read a book he held in his lap.

Seized by a fit of anger, Fetterman reached over, grabbed the flashlight, flicked it off and flung it to the ground. "You idiot." Then in a conciliatory tone he added, "Sir."

Carrington defended his action. "It's dark out. How in hell am I supposed to see?"

"Think before you act."

The argument was interrupted by the sounds of battle. An American soldier manning the perimeter defenses fired an illuminating flare, and the shooting began.

The NVA regulars came in wider waves more frequently than before. They ran and yelled at the top of their voices, throwing grenades and firing rapidly. Their bayonets were fixed, but they never got close enough to use them.

The machine gunners and the mortar crews did most of the killing for the Americans. Machine gun fire raked the hillside in a swell that ranged from six inches to three feet. In spite of it, the NVA soldiers surged across the open ground, making themselves easy targets. A few of them reached the wire before they were hit, but nobody crossed the barbed strands. Fetterman estimated there was at least a battalion of NVA regulars attacking.

Their fire was growing more intense and more accurate by the minute. Bullets sped by overhead; one shattered the black plastic foregrip of the lieutenant's M-16. Another bullet nicked his helmet, spinning it sideways on his head. He continued firing as fast as he could shove magazines into his weapon. When he spotted five enemy soldiers running toward a dropped RPD machine gun, he stood, riddled them with fire and flopped down again. He hit the ground just in time to avoid a burst of AK fire.

And then as suddenly as it had begun, the battle ended as the NVA melted into the tree line.

"Cease fire! Cease fire!" screamed Fetterman. "Cease fucking fire!" He was concerned they would foolishly use up all of their ammunition.

"Well, how'd we do?" asked Carrington.

"Round two, we did okay," said Fetterman. "It's too soon to tell about round three."

THE MOON SHONE BRIGHT overhead and the stars twinkled, giving the starlight scope plenty of ambient light to gather and amplify. Fetterman stared in disbelief through the hand-held night vision scope at a sapper who was busily worming his way through the concertina wire instead of snipping through the strands with wire cutters. The sapper was making progress as easily as if the barrier were tall grass instead of razor-sharp steel.

Fetterman marveled at his foe's agility and his ignorance that he was under surveillance. The master sergeant wondered what the enemy would do if he found out he was being watched. Would he ignore the fact and keep crawling inexorably toward his objective, or panic, jump to his feet and make a run for it? Unaware of his predicament, the sapper did neither. He cleared the wire and halted next to a claymore mine.

Fetterman knew the sapper, if given the opportunity, would uproot the mine and turn it around so that when detonated its fusillade of stainless-steel balls would riddle American soldiers and not the attackers.

Fetterman grimaced. It would be a waste of a perfectly good claymore mine to take just one enemy life, but it was unavoidable. He reached for the firing handle. "Say good night, Charlie."

A fraction of a second later the flat bang traversed the killing field, reverberated off the tree line and echoed back across the camp. From somewhere across the broad expanse of the compound a flare went up, illuminating the landscape with its surrealistic orange light. Shielding the night scope's sensitive optics from the brilliant glow in the sky, Fetterman looked across the open ground to where a bundle of bloodied black rags hung in the concertina. The brutal force of the claymore expansion had mangled the sapper and hurled the remnants of his body back into the wire he had so painstakingly negotiated.

Outraged by their comrade's death, the enemy started firing. The orange glow of the flare burned as brightly as a small sun, its harsh rays illuminating the battleground and casting an eerie light over the scenery, lending it the look and feel of an alien starscape.

Yet Fetterman barely noticed the light show. After viewing the pyrotechnics of modern warfare so many times, he was no longer impressed by them.

Fetterman picked up an M-16 and started firing at the tree line where the muzzle-flashes winked like fireflies. None of the enemy had yet left their cover. When the flare died down, so did the firing.

AT FOUR A.M. a jagged burst of machine gun fire shattered the silence, the ruby-red tracers lazily arcing their way toward the tree line. Then it was silent.

PFC Alan Watts, the ex-rock and roll drummer, figured someone was getting edgy. Watts figured the man had seen something move in the barbed wire outside, an understandable overreaction given the circumstances.

He lay on his back just outside the machine gun bunker, staring at the sky. It was a beautiful night, with a gentle breeze that felt cool against his sweaty skin. Then out of the darkness came the clattering of an empty C-ration can. His heart seemed to stop.

An ominous sound came from the direction of the jungle—a single incoming mortar round. Watts rolled over onto his belly and crawled into his hole. A moment later there was an ear-splitting crash and a burst of flames. The ground shook under him and rubble pelted the side of the bunker. A cloud of dust tickled his nose. After a few seconds he raised his head. The dust thrown up by the explosion was settling, but the smell of the detonated mortar round still hung heavy in the air and made his nose run.

Then a flare went up and he saw dozens of enemy soldiers running across the open ground. Watts jumped into the pit, and he and his loader commenced firing, unleashing three- and four-round bursts. There were so many attackers that they started stretching out into ten- and twenty-round bursts.

Watts lost track of how many 250-round belts of ammunition had been expended. The heavy machine gun looked as if it had been in a fire, the barrel burned orange and flaking. As he continued to shoot, the muzzle-flash attracted more and more attention until it seemed Watts's bunker was the only target.

As bullets splattered against the sandbags around him, he unfastened the traversing mechanism and crouched low, sighting along the underside of the barrel so that no part of him was visible above the level of the gun. Hand over his head, he hung on to the butterfly trigger and raked the ground in front of him.

ON THE OTHER SIDE of the compound in the stone house command post, Carrington suddenly had a bright idea. "The .50-caliber sniper rifle. Couldn't we adjust it so it fires fully automatic again?"

"You're right," said Fetterman. "Good thinking. Come on."

The two of them took off, running in a half crouch when Fetterman heard the loud whoosh of a rocket and shoved Carrington hard into a bomb crater. The explosion blew away a foot and a half of the crater's rim, leaving Fetterman dazed and the lieutenant half buried beneath a pile of dirt. Fetterman pulled Carrington out unhurt.

The master sergeant got to his feet, took a step and felt his ankles tangle in something. He reached down, and by the light of the next exploding mortar round could see that his legs had become entwined in someone's intestines. Carrington helped free him from the grisly bonds.

"Maybe we should wait until the firing slacks off," the lieutenant said. "Then we can press Staley's .50 into service."

Fetterman nodded, and they began to work their way back to the safety of the stone house.

A shell exploded nearby with a great crash. Earth and flame mushroomed toward the sky. Instinctively Carrington ducked, his hand protecting his head. After a few moments he stood, spitting dirt. He looked across at Fetterman in time to see the master sergeant blinking with dust-rimmed eyes. Under a shelter twenty yards away a small pile of ammunition was on fire. A soldier ran over to the burning ammo and yanked off the burning tent. A barrage of mortar rounds detonated, catching him unaware. The ground shuddered as Carrington once more dropped onto his stomach. There was a loud scream as the man vanished from a direct hit.

Deciding they'd never make it to the deuce-and-a-half, let alone be able to modify the weapon under fire, they gave it up and retreated to the cover of the stone house.

THREE HUNDRED FEET away from Fetterman and Carrington, Snowflake crouched low in his bunker. Directly in front of him, small-arms fire crackled inside the tree line. Blue-green tracers flew overhead. Suddenly his eyes were filled with a white light, and a deafening roar hurt his eardrums as an explosion picked him up and hurled him hard onto his back. A body spun through the air over Snowflake's head. Blood and dirt sprayed the cook. Even before he got up again, he knew that his buddy was dead.

"He's dead!" screamed Snowflake. "You dirty fucking Commie bastards!" Angrily he got to his feet and felt around for his M-16. When he found it, he slapped a fresh twenty-round magazine into it. With deliberate shots he started picking off the blurry figures as they advanced from the tree line. "Die, you motherfuckers, die!" His buddy had been the first man he had ever seen killed.

By this time some of the enemy had made it through the wire and were loose in the compound. Disregarding the danger, the angry American came out of the hole to meet the enemy. One of the intruders raised his AK-47 to the firing position, but Snowflake drilled him through the chest. He fell forward, dead before he hit the ground.

Three more NVA soldiers sprang up from cover, firing at Snowflake as they rushed forward. Two died in their tracks. The third whirled and started running toward the jungle, catching someone's stray bullet in the back.

18

**IN THE JUNGLE NEAR
ELEPHANT EAR
CAMBODIA**

Captain Gerber was lying in his jungle hammock recalling the events of the previous night when Krung had killed Chuyen. As he lay there feeling the tightness in his calf muscles just beginning to subside, the sky turned orange. Instantly he recognized it as an illuminating flare off to the west. Then came the inevitable crackle of small-arms fires: M-16s, M-60s and AK-47s slugging it out. The Green Beret captain uttered a single word, ''Fetterman.''

Intuitively he knew that the master sergeant was part of the conflict. The intensity of the light from the flare, and the nearness of the sound, indicated to Gerber that the battle was about two klicks away.

He woke the camp, mobilizing the troops as rapidly as he could. He had a feeling that time was critical, so they stuck to the trails. For the sake of speed he decided to take some risks, hoping they wouldn't trigger a booby trap.

An hour later, when they were close to the fighting, they slowed down, knowing full well they were likely to run into the rear guard of the NVA battle force. Lying hidden at the edge of a tree line, Gerber tried to control his breathing from the exertion. From his position he could survey the scent of battle without danger. The jungle reverberated with the sounds of war as the NVA and the Americans traded bullets. Red tracers lanced out from Firebase Rio Indio in exchange for green ones hurrying back in. Bursts of automatic rifle fire punctuated the night air.

Gerber called Walsh to his side and told him to tune in a particular frequency, explaining that he and Fetterman had worked it out years before. If one needed to contact the other and no frequency had been assigned, they would use their secret one.

A moment later Fetterman and Gerber made contact. "Can't talk long," said the master sergeant. "I'm kind of busy right now. I got a bunch of guys in my front yard shooting at me, trying to kill me. Musta done something to piss 'em off. Over."

"Roger that," said Gerber. "I'm down the street about a klick, watching it all go down. You want any help, or you figure you can handle this squabble all by yourself? Over."

The radio was silent for a minute. A moment later came the dull roar of an exploding mortar round inside the compound. "That one was too close," said Fetterman. "Do what you can to draw fire. We're into it up to our ears. By the way, if you get in, watch out for the foogas. I'm letting it roll in one-zero minutes. Over."

"Roger, roger, roger. Out."

In five minutes Gerber had assessed the situation. The NVA no longer encircled the camp; they had massed their forces for a frontal assault. And the best way to help the defenders was by means of a modified flanking maneuver he called double coyote ugly. Gerber and his men would stay on the move, assaulting the enemy, then melt away into the shadows, like a pack of coyotes hitting and running, hitting and running.

Gerber gathered his men around him and explained the plan. In the desert regions of the American Southwest a pack of coyotes would circle a man until one of the animals got a chance to sneak up behind him and nip at his ankle. The man would whirl to get away and another dog would come up from behind him and also bite him on the ankle. Instinctively the man would start spinning around and around in an attempt to save his shredded ankles. Soon he'd be dizzy, and then it was a matter of time before he fell to the ground and the coyotes went for his throat.

Gerber was out to play coyote with the NVA. He finished up by saying, "Let's go for the throat, gentlemen."

They dumped their rucksacks into a pile where they could find them again, and only carrying arms and ammunition, spread out in a skirmish line, advancing toward the enemy. When they got close enough to see the NVA soldiers silhouetted against the blaze of light from the expended ordnance, the Americans dropped to the ground and fired at full-auto, two magazines each. Then they ceased fire and crawled away to repeat the exercise from another position. The NVA unit was like an angry bear attacking a fresh kill, with a pack of coyotes nipping at its heel.

Walsh fought with the radio clicked on, the volume cranked wide open and one earphone draped over his head. "Foogas in the hole," he screamed to the others.

In preparation for the attack, Fetterman had mixed gasoline and oil in fifty-five-gallon drums, and now he was about to unleash the weapon on the enemy.

"Don't look directly at it when it goes off or it will ruin your night vision," reminded Gerber as he and the others ducked. They watched as fifty-five-gallon drums started rolling down the hill and picked up more and more speed.

The NVA troopers deftly sidestepped the big black drums and virtually ignored them as they rolled into their midst.

For a moment the rifle fire coming from the American emplacements seemed to concentrate on the drums. In horror the NVA realized what was going on, and they started running for the tree line. One by one the drums full of gasoline and motor oil exploded in the middle of the enemy soldiers. The brilliant reddish-orange fireball engulfed dozens of men. Some of them screamed in agony as burning liquid splattered them, the oil in the flames clinging to their burning skin. The ones who inhaled the flames simply fell to the ground.

When the brilliant intensity of the flames died down, Gerber gave the command, "Now!" The end of the battle was a turkey shoot. Some of the men took potshots. Walsh raked the enemy in a full-auto burst, wishing he could take down two and three men with each bullet. Wisely, the scattered remnants of what was left of the NVA force retreated into the trees.

"Coyote, huh, Captain Gerber?" Walsh commented.

Gerber nodded. "Coyote."

GERBER AND FETTERMAN stood over the thing but seemed oblivious to its presence. The thing was a man's body from the waist down, the legs and hips swollen by decomposition, the bloated features straining at the seams of the black pajama pants, threatening to burst them wide open.

"We had a close call last night," said Fetterman, pulling his hand across his face. His eyes were ringed black from lack of sleep. His dirty fatigues further attested to the strain of battle.

The two of them surveyed the area. It stank with bloated corpses and was littered with the ubiquitous debris of war: bloody pith helmets and bullet-riddled AK stocks and canteens. In a fit of anger, Gerber kicked an American helmet that had been creased by a bullet.

"Count your men, Uncle Ho," said Fetterman.

Lieutenant Carrington joined the two Special Forces men, and as the trio surveyed the battlefield, Gerber observed that some of the wounded had no chance for medical attention. During the heaviest fighting the air had been thick with grenade fragments and tracer bullets, so the wounded had lain in their holes and some of them had bled to death.

Carrington found a sandy-haired, clean-cut kid who must have been badly wounded by a grenade earlier in the attack. The lieutenant figured he had bled all night but kept firing his machine gun until he grew too weak to press the butterfly trigger. Four dead VC were found around his hole.

Fetterman's tone was grave. "Looks like rock and roll has lost a drummer."

They walked to the stone house, where they had set up the temporary morgue for the American dead. It had taken a beating. The entire length of stone wall was pockmarked, little chips knocked out by rifle and machine gun bullets, larger chips knocked out by heavy machine gun fire. A B-40 rocket had knocked a big hole clean through the wall. Three Americans had died outside the house when the rocket had exploded.

Like an old West gunfighter who had killed too many men in shoot-outs, Carrington felt like hanging up his guns. He felt an overwhelming guilt at having killed another human being. He also felt guilty because he had faced another mortal on equal terms and walked away the victor. "I killed a man last night," he said morosely to Fetterman and Gerber.

You're wrong, thought Fetterman. He had seen the lieutenant shoot at least a dozen, but he still knew what the man was talking about.

"Look," said Fetterman, "it's one less enemy who can sneak up on you and kill you. And you and he went one-on-one, and he fucking lost. So don't feel bad about killing. Waste of time to load yourself down with all that extra baggage. It invites hesitation the next time, and as a result it could be some Commie standing over your body, gloating."

Snowflake stumbled in with a stunned expression on his face, bumping into Captain Gerber as if he hadn't even seen him.

Gerber turned on the cook angrily. "Jesus, what's wrong with you, soldier? Are you shell-shocked, drunk or on drugs?"

Walsh came running in behind Snowflake and breathlessly said, "We were listening to rock and roll and the prick 74 when the news came on . . ."

Snowflake's expression reminded Gerber of a sleepwalker. His voice was a monotone. "They've shot Reverend King. They've shot Martin Luther King." He talked very rapidly in an agitated voice. "This is the white man's way. They send us over here to get out of the slums so we won't riot and hope Charlie kills a bunch of us. And those that stay home the police kill with nightsticks. And our leaders are assassinated by the KKK and the Nazis. Goddamn, I want to give Charlie more bullets to help him kill more honkies."

19

THE CONTINENTAL SHELF HOTEL SAIGON, RVN

Gerber and Fetterman were seated at the sidewalk café, sipping orange juice and eating runny eggs when the waiter came over to inform them they had an urgent call waiting at the front desk. It was the duty officer at Nha Trang. A Colonel Crawley had radioed in from his Huey en route from Bien Hoa to tell them they should pick him up at the helipad.

The two men finished their meal, then jumped into their Jeep, arriving at the helipad just as the UH-1D was settling onto its skids. Sergeant Dirty Shirt Crawley jumped out and trotted over.

Fetterman gave Dirty Shirt a good-natured jab on the shoulder. "Congratulations on the promotion, Colonel."

"Thanks, Tony," replied Dirty Shirt.

"So how did it go back in the World?" asked Gerber diplomatically. He didn't want to talk about Sergeant Johnson's funeral directly. He'd let Dirty Shirt bring it up if he needed to.

"Goddamn," he told them breathlessly. "They call it the real world, but it ain't. It's fucking goofy."

Fetterman had the North Vietnamese flag he had captured in the recent battle wadded up in a ball and tucked under his arm, while Dirty Shirt had the American flag from Johnson's funeral neatly folded and tucked in his. The two of them looked at each other, and at each other's flag.

Fetterman shrugged at the irony.

Dirty Shirt pointed at Fetterman's flag.

"Border work," Gerber explained. "We've been busy working on the immigrant problem from the North while you've been gone."

"Anybody seriously hurt?"

"We're clean, but Chuyen decided to stay in Cambodia and send us detailed reports. He's with the underground, if you get my drift."

"Good. I never trusted that son of a bitch from the day I laid eyes on him," Dirty Shirt growled.

Fetterman grinned. "You're not alone, brother. So tell us about your trip. What's cooking back in the land of the free and the home of the brave?"

Dirty Shirt shook his head. "Goddamn civilians. It didn't go so good. The first American I saw in Oakland called me a murderer and a warmonger. Second one called me a baby killer." He paused for effect before continuing. "Then he spit on me."

Gerber's face darkened. "I'd heard it was getting more than a little out of hand. So what did you do?"

"I turned the proverbial other cheek."

"Good. You did the right thing. If you had hit him in the nose, you'd have felt better, but it would have only proven his point. Although I wouldn't think any less of you if you had paid some wino to crack him over the head with a wine bottle and gouge his eyes out with the shards of glass. Just kidding.''

"Like I said, I turned the other cheek, but that didn't end it,'' he said wryly. "He wouldn't let go.''

"So what happened?''

"He was so pissed off that he couldn't get to me that he took a swing. Sucker punch. Missed of course.''

"So what did you do?'' Gerber wasn't sure he really wanted to know.

Dirty Shirt shrugged. "Under the circumstances I did the only thing I could. I didn't want to do it, but he forced me.''

Gerber played along. "Okay. I'll bite. What did you do?''

"I killed him.''

Gerber knew Dirty Shirt well enough to know he had been putting them on. "Uh-huh. So how's it feel to be back in-country?'' he asked.

Dirty Shirt thought before answering, remembering the string of unpleasant encounters, beginning with the old lady with the blue hair, the hippie and his chick and the thousand-pound bimbo in the fur coat who had wanted to bang him in the rest room. And how all that had been balanced out by the old man who had bought his breakfast, and Cindy, the blonde with the airline who had seated him in the first-class cabin.

For the first time in his life Dirty Shirt could see he was only really at home with men who had shared hardship and deprivation with him in the field. His life-style was something civilians couldn't relate to. In their estimation they stacked up as lost, weak and helpless creatures, especially when compared to men like Gerber and Fetterman. Civilians talked big but never had the courage to back up their words, because once they took that chance they faced the possibility of death.

Finally Dirty Shirt said, "It's good to be home, Captain. Good to be in a situation where all I own is my M-16, my rucksack and an extra beret, and I know I can count on the men around me."

20

IN THE JUNGLE SOMEWHERE IN CAMBODIA

The morning after the battle Dinh shook Morrow and Maxwell awake. "You are going home," he told them.

The two Americans couldn't believe their ears. One-Eye would escort them first by truck, then by jungle trail to the Cambodian village where they had originally been captured. And while the two Americans were relieved to learn their captivity was nearly over, the thought of another wearying day on the trail didn't excite them. Nonetheless, there was no question about accepting their freedom.

"There never was a Norwood," Dinh told Morrow. "We used our agents to spread the rumor of his existence and later employed the services of a Russian military adviser in a number of battles." He shrugged. "Once a rumor starts it has wings of its own. When the American soldiers saw the Russian, he became your Norwood."

Maxwell's tone was controlled but still angry. "So you set us up, hoping we journalists would fall for it and you could lure us into Cambodia where you could capture us. And then we'd be compelled to tell the war story from the NVA point of view. After all, how could we resist telling all about our dramatic adventure?''

Amused, Dinh could barely contain himself. "Almost, my CIA friend. We know exactly who you are, and we have known from the start. In fact, from the moment the two of you set foot in the helicopter at Hotel Three. We even know you argued briefly with the pilot, the one with the mongoose killer. We have eyes and ears everywhere, but especially at American installations.''

Maxwell seemed wary of Dinh. "So where does that leave things?''

"Simple. Not only will Morrow tell the world what she has seen and heard over the past few days, but you will tell your experiences to all of the other spies in Saigon. You have learned nothing of strategic importance. We have seen to that. If you have seen one jungle trail, you have seen them all. You see, you are more valuable to us alive than dead. The more you and Morrow talk, the better. And given the nature of both of your professions, neither of you will be able to control your tongues.''

Dinh turned his head at the sound of a truck rumbling into the village. It stopped outside the hut. "Have a safe journey," he told them. "Oh, and Mr. Maxwell, next time I'm in Saigon, I'd like to meet for coffee to talk over old times with you. But you'll understand if I don't.''

One-Eye was strangely silent throughout the trip. He rode in the cab with the driver and made Morrow and Maxwell ride in the back. There was no guard. Morrow figured the reasoning was simple: why would they try to escape when they were on their way home?

After a couple of hours on bumpy roads, the Czech-made truck pulled over to the side. One-Eye stayed in the cab, stuck his head out the window and yelled for them to get out. The two Americans hopped over the tailgate and walked around the side of the truck where One-Eye's arm hung out of the window. He wouldn't meet their gaze, but pointed to the edge of the jungle and the beginning of a narrow vine-choked trail. "You walk two hours. Come to village," he grunted.

"You were supposed to guide us to the village," said Morrow defiantly. She figured One-Eye was being lazy and was probably going to spend that time in a whorehouse somewhere along the road instead of making sure they got safely to their destination.

He turned to stare at her with his one good eye. After a moment he broke into a grin. "I was also supposed to kill your friend, Maxwell. Dinh not like him. But I like *you*." He waggled a finger at her. "You owe me big. You write story all about me. Brave jungle fighter." Then he turned to Maxwell. "You one lucky son of a bitch. She not your friend, you dead."

Before Maxwell could answer, One-Eye shouted at the driver and motioned for him to go. The driver ground the gears and let out the clutch. The truck lurched, kicking up a cloud of gravel from its rear tires, then started down the road, leaving them to choke on the dust.

Maxwell kicked at the gravel. Once the truck had disappeared, they edged into the jungle. Maxwell wanted to run along the trail and make the best time they could, but Morrow knew they should pace themselves. One-Eye had said it was a two-hour trek, but it could end up being more like four or five. And they didn't have any water. Morrow cursed herself for not having thought of it earlier.

An hour into the jungle they took a break and sat on a thick tree trunk that had fallen across the trail. Sweating profusely, Morrow wiped her shirtsleeve across her forehead. Seeing motion out of the corner of her eye, she instinctively turned to see what it was. About fifty feet away was a family of cobras, big ones and little ones, bunched together in the tall grass and upright, craning their necks at Morrow and Maxwell.

"Come on, Jerry," she said. "Maybe you're right. Let's not run, but let's at least pick up the pace."

Once at the village, they waited in the thatched pavilion. One of the women gave them water and a tiny portion of rice. Sitting on their haunches, sharing the rice between them, they enjoyed the slight breeze that made the midday heat a little more bearable. Morrow realized they were sitting in the wide-legged squat, just like the Vietnamese and Cambodians, and wondered how many other traits she had picked up during her captivity.

Morrow heard the helicopter first and almost ran for cover. Catching herself she chuckled and kidded Maxwell about how they would need to decompress. Walking outside, she had to shield her eyes from the harsh sunlight as she searched the sky for the source of the sound.

Maxwell's eyes were keener. "There it is," he called out, hoping his voice hadn't cracked and betrayed his elation.

After a few moments scanning the cloudless blue sky, Morrow saw it, too, a black Huey flying just above the horizon, losing altitude fast and closing on their position. It was just like the one that had brought them into Cambodia in the first place. She wondered if the pilot was Mickey.

She started looking on the ground for a plume of sulfureous red or purple smoke from a smoke grenade that would tell the pilot their whereabouts as well as direction of the wind. But there wasn't any. Then she realized that only American troops would pop smoke on an LZ, and out in the boonies it was just her, Maxwell and the hot wind.

Gently touching its skids, then settling its full weight down, the aircraft landed in the clearing. Mickey, the Air America pilot, walked toward them. With a smirk on his face, he said to Maxwell, "You again, huh?" He ignored Robin. His lanky copilot stood next to him, smiling.

Morrow noticed Mickey's arm was red and swollen, with purple streaks running from wrist to elbow. The two black indentations in his skin that looked like fang marks were what worried her the most. "My God, what did you do to your arm?" she blurted out. "That looks like a snakebite."

An embarrassed shrug was his only reply.

Morrow expressed her concern. "I'd have a doctor look at it if I were you. It doesn't look healthy."

His face held the expression of a man who wanted to tell her to go fuck herself, but he bit his tongue instead.

"He already did see a doc," said the copilot. "Sam the Sham got pissed off and bit him. Again. No big deal." Then he guffawed, "If a cobra had bitten him, it'd be a different story. He'd be deader than a whore's heart, that's for sure."

Mouth agape, Morrow asked the copilot how he could be so nonchalant about something as serious as a snakebite.

He shrugged. "Mickey's always getting bitten. First time he nearly died. No joke. Second time he was deathly ill. Third time he just lay around in his hotel room for a coupla days, moaning and groaning. Shoot, whenever he gets nipped by those fangs now, it just gives him a headache and makes him one mean son of a bitch to work around. Hell, I got a big bet going back in Saigon with all the other pilots says next time the rattler bites Mickey, the snake's gonna take sick, curl up in a corner and die."

Morrow turned to Maxwell. "You people keep strange company," she murmured.

Maxwell gave her an exaggerated smile in return.

By then Mickey had wandered off into the village, presumably to find somebody with a mongoose and friends with faith in its serpent-slaying abilities. Ten minutes later he came back, walking fast, with a gaggle of Cambodians hot on his heels. Mickey was grinning as he walked to the cargo compartment and grabbed the familiar burlap bag.

Watching his actions, Morrow remarked, "He's not very careful with the snake. No wonder he's been bitten so many times."

By then the Cambodians had formed a circle on the shady side of the chopper. Morrow looked on as a man in his thirties stood at one end of the crowd, cuddling a mongoose and affectionately rubbing its wet nose. Like a common house cat, its tongue flicked out and it began to lick the man's lips. Morrow recalled how she had seen a mother mongoose gnawing on a cobra's head, and suddenly she felt nauseous.

Mickey unceremoniously dumped his rattler onto the ground and then jumped clear as Sam feigned a little strike at his boots. "Fuck you, rattler," said Mickey, walking away.

And then the ill-tempered rattler slithered toward the center of the clearing as if he knew exactly what was expected of him. Once he found his spot, he stopped and waited for the mongoose.

Mickey looked worried when he told Maxwell, "The villagers tell me this is one bad-news mongoose. Translated from Cambodian, his name means Famed Killer of Serpents."

"Sammy always wins," Maxwell commented.

The mongoose padded up to within a short distance of the snake, then paused for a moment as it sized up its foe. After a few moments, it leaned its long, slender body forward, seemingly straining to keep its clawed feet planted in the earth and still lean as far forward as possible toward the snake. All the while the animal chattered, as if insulting the snake, bobbing and weaving, intentionally provoking the rattler, daring him to strike.

Sam just lay there, unimpressed by the show. Suddenly he struck, but the mongoose took a quick step backward, avoiding the fangs. Sam recoiled.

The crowd started chattering, having heard stories about the man in the black helicopter and his invincible cobra without a hood. They also knew young and inexperienced mongooses were often killed by snakes, and that the ones that survived were savvy and agile. This mongoose was older and trained, and they knew the battle could go either way.

Recovered from its near brush with death, the mongoose resumed taunting the serpent. Again, leaning forward and chattering away at the snake, it tried to provoke Sam into a strike.

The snake shook his rattles, the sound sending cold shivers up and down Morrow's spine. Speed blurred the image as Sam struck out, extending his long body to its limit. But the mongoose's fancy footwork once more allowed it to avoid the jaws of death. As Sam came forward, the mongoose merely sidestepped and sprung at Sam's head in an attempt to climb onto his back and bite his skull before the snake could recoil. But Sam was too fast. By the time the mongoose got there, the snake had already recoiled.

Warily the mongoose padded back and forth. Again Sam struck with lightning speed. This time he caught the little mongoose off guard. Sam sunk his fangs into the side of the rodent's body. The creature shrieked as Sam recoiled. The crowd was deathly silent as the mongoose started quivering. In less than a minute it lay still, then Sam started to slither over. The crowd was silent and unmoving as Sam opened his jaw wide and started to swallow his prey.

The owner stepped out of the crowd and started over to pull the mongoose from the rattler's jaws.

Mickey held out a hand and called out in a loud voice, "I wouldn't if I were you. He's hungry."

The mongoose's owner nodded and, not wanting to suffer the same fall as his creature, just stood there in dismay. Sam swallowed the mongoose whole, and the lump started working its way down the length of his body.

After a while Mickey walked up to the snake, stood over him and started to scold. "I'm tired of your angry temperament, Sam. You're worse than my third wife. Things are going to change *muy pronto*." With that, Mickey brought the heel of his snakeskin cowboy boot down on the back of Sam's neck. He ground his heel against the serpent as if he were putting out a cigarette butt. Morrow could hear the crunch of bone as Mickey smashed the snake's skull. Then he calmly whirled around and headed for the helicopter, calling after him, "I'm on my way to Saigon. Anybody going along better get on board. I want to catch a flight to Hong Kong later tonight, and time's awastin'."

Morrow looked at Maxwell. "Like I told you before, Jerry, you guys keep strange company."

GLOSSARY

AC—Aircraft Commander. The pilot in charge of the aircraft.

ADO—A-Detachment's area of operations.

AFVN—Armed Forces radio and television network in Vietnam. Army PFC Pat Sajak was probably the most memorable of AFVN's DJs with his loud and long, "GOOOOOOOOOOOOD MORNing, Vietnam!" The spinning Wheel of Fortune gives no clues about his whereabouts today.

AK-47—Assault rifle normally used by the North Vietnamese and the Vietcong.

AO—Area of Operations.

AO DAI—Long dresslike garment, split up the sides and worn over pants.

AP ROUNDS—Armor-piercing ammunition.

APU—Auxiliary Power Unit. An outside source of power used to start aircraft engines.

ARC LIGHT—Term used for a B-52 bombing mission. It was also known as heavy arty.

ARVN—Army of the Republic of Vietnam. A South Vietnamese soldier. Also known as Marvin Arvin.

ASA—Army Security Agency. Electronic intelligence gatherers.

AST—Control officer between men in isolation and the outside world. He is responsible for taking care of all problems.

AUTOVON—Army phone system that allowed soldiers on one base to call another base, bypassing the civilian phone system.

BISCUIT—C-rations.

BODY COUNT—Number of enemy killed, wounded or captured during an operation. Used by Saigon and Washington as a means of measuring progress of the war.

BOOM-BOOM—Term used by Vietnamese prostitutes in selling their services.

BOONDOGGLE—Any military operation that hasn't been completely thought out. An operation that is ridiculous.

BOONIE HAT—Soft cap worn by a grunt in the field when not wearing his steel pot.

BREAK STARCH—To don freshly starched fatigues.

C AND C—Command and Control aircraft that circled overhead to direct combined air and ground operations.

CAO BOI—Cowboys. Term that referred to the criminals of Saigon who rode motorcycles.

CARIBOU—Cargo transport plane.

CHINOOK—Army Aviation twin-engine helicopter. A CH-47. See also SHIT HOOK.

CHOCK—Term referring to the number of the aircraft in the flight. Chock Three was the third. Chock Six was the sixth.

CLAYMORE—Antipersonnel mine that fires seven hundred and fifty steel balls with a lethal range of fifty meters.

CLOSE AIR SUPPORT—Use of airplanes and helicopters to fire on enemy units near friendly troops.

CO CONG—Female Vietcong.

CONEX—Steel container about ten feet high, ten feet deep and ten feet long used to haul equipment and supplies.

DAI UY—Vietnamese army rank equivalent to captain.

DEROS—Date of Estimated Return from Overseas Service.

DF—Direction Finder.

DIRNSA—Director, National Security Agency.

E-6—Staff sergeant.

E AND E—Escape and Evasion.

FAC—Forward air controller.

FEET WET—Term used by pilots to describe flight over water.

FIVE—Radio call sign for the executive officer of a unit.

FNG—Fucking New Guy.

FOB—Forward Operating Base.

FOOGAS—Jellied gasoline similar to napalm.

FOX MIKE—FM radio.

FREEDOM BIRD—Name given to any aircraft that took troops out of Vietnam. Usually referred to the commercial jet flights that took men back to the World.

GARAND—The M-1 rifle that was replaced by the M-14.

GO-TO-HELL RAG—Towel or any large cloth worn around the neck by a grunt.

GRAIL—NATO name for the shoulder-fired SA-7 surface-to-air missile.

GREASE GUN—See M-3A1.

GUARD THE RADIO—Stand by in the commo bunker and listen for messages.

GUIDELINE—NATO name for SA-2 surface-to-air missile.

HE—High-explosive ammunition.

HOOTCH—Almost any shelter, from temporary to long-term.

HORN—Term referring to a specific kind of radio operations that used satellites to rebroadcast messages.

HORSE—See BISCUIT.

HOTEL THREE—Helicopter landing area at Saigon's Tan Son Nhut Airport.

HUEY—UH-1 helicopter.

IN-COUNTRY—Term used to refer to American troops operating in South Vietnam. They were all in-country.

INTELLIGENCE—Any information about enemy operations. It could include troops movements, weapons capabilities, biographies of enemy commanders and general information about terrain features. Any information that would be useful in planning a mission.

KA-BAR—Type of military combat knife with a sharp blade and a blood groove.

KIA—Killed In Action. (Since the U.S. wasn't engaged in a declared war, the use of the term KIA wasn't authorized. KIA came to mean enemy dead. Americans were KHA—Killed in Hostile action.)

KLICK—One thousand meters. A kilometer.

LIMA LIMA—Land line. Refers to telephone communications between two points on the ground.

LLDB—Luc Luong Dac Biet. The South Vietnamese Special Forces. Sometimes referred to as the Look Long, Duck Back.

LP—Listening Post. A position outside the perimeter manned by a couple of soldiers to give advance warning of enemy activity.

LSA—Lubricant used by soldiers on their weapons to ensure they would continue to operate properly.

LZ—Landing zone.

M-3A1—Also known as a grease gun. A .45-caliber submachine gun favored in World War II by GIs because its slow rate of fire meant that the barrel didn't rise and that they didn't burn through their ammo as fast as with some other weapons.

M-14—Standard rifle of the U.S. Army, eventually replaced by the M-16. It fires the standard NATO round—7.62 mm.

M-16—Standard infantry weapon of the Vietnam War. It fires 5.56 mm ammunition.

M-79—Short-barreled, shoulder-fired weapon that fires a 40 mm grenade. These can be high explosives, white phosphorus or canister.

MACV—Military Assistance Command, Vietnam. Replaced MAAG in 1964.

MEDEVAC—Helicopter used to take wounded to medical facilities. Also called Dust-off.

MIA—Missing In Action.

MONOPOLY MONEY—Term describing MPC handed out in lieu of regular U.S. currency.

MOS—Military Occupation Specialty. A job description.

MPC—Military Payment Certificates. The monopoly money used instead of real cash.

NCO—Noncommissioned officer. A noncom. A sergeant.

NCOIC—NCO In Charge. The senior NCO in a unit, detachment or patrol.

NDB—Nondirectional Beacon. A radio beacon that can be used for homing.

NEXT—The man who was the next to be rotated home. See SHORT.

NINETEEN—Average age of combat soldier in Vietnam, as opposed to twenty-six in World War II.

NOUC-MAM—Foul-smelling sauce used by Vietnamese.

NVA—North Vietnamese Army. Also used to designate a soldier from North Vietnam.

OD—Olive drab. The color the U.S. Army paints everything.

P(PIASTER)—Basic monetary unit in South Vietnam, worth slightly less than a penny.

PETA-PRIME—Tarlike substance that melted in the heat of the day to become a sticky black nightmare that clung to boots, clothes and equipment. It was used to hold down dust during the dry season.

PLF—Parachute Landing Fall. The roll used by parachutists on landing.

POW—Prisoner of War.

PRC-10—Portable radio

PRC-25—Portable radio, lighter than the PRC-10, which it replaced.

PULL PITCH—Term used by helicopter pilots, meaning they are going to take off.

PUNJI STAKE—Sharpened bamboo hidden to penetrate the foot. Sometimes dipped in feces.

PUZZLE PALACE—Term referring to the Pentagon, because no one knew what was going on in it. Puzzle Palace East referred to MACV or USARV Headquarters in Saigon.

RINGKNOCKER—Graduate of a military academy. The term refers to the class ring worn by all graduates.

RON—Remain Overnight. Term used by flight crews to indicate a flight that would last longer than a day.

RPD—Light Soviet machine gun—7.62 mm.

RTO—Radio Telephone Operator. The radio man of a unit.

SA-2—Surface-to-air missile fired from a fixed site. It is a radar-guided missile that is nearly thirty-five feet long.

SA-7—Surface-to-air missile that is shoulder-fired and has infrared homing.

SACSA—Special Assistant for Counterinsurgency and Special Activities.

SAFE AREA—Selected Area For Evasion. It doesn't mean that the area is safe from the enemy, only that the terrain, location or local population make the area a good place for escape and evasion.

SAM TWO—Term referring to the SA-2 Guideline.

SAR—Search and Rescue. SAR forces were the people involved in search-and-rescue missions.

SFOB—Special Forces Operational Base.

SHIT HOOK—Name applied by the troops to the Chinook helicopter because of all the "shit" stirred up by its massive rotors.

SHORT—Term used by someone in Vietnam to tell all who would listen that his tour was almost over.

SHORT-TIME—GI term for a quickie.

SHORT-TIMER—Person who had been in Vietnam for nearly a year and who would be rotated back to the World soon. When his DEROS was the shortest in the unit, the person was said to be next.

SINGLE-DIGIT MIDGET—Soldier with fewer than ten days left in-country.

SIX—Radio call sign for the unit commander.

SKS—Soviet-made carbine.

SMG—Submachine gun.

SOI—Signal Operating Instructions. The booklet that contained the call signs and radio frequencies of the units in Vietnam.

SOP—Standard Operating Procedure.

SPIKE TEAM—Special Forces team made up for a direct-action mission.

SSB—Single Sideband—method of radio signal transmission.

STEEL POT—Standard U.S. Army helmet. The steel pot was the outer metal cover.

TEAM UNIFORM OR COMPANY UNIFORM—UHF radio frequency on which the team or the company communicates. Frequencies were changed periodically in an attempt to confuse the enemy.

TDY—Termporary duty, temporary assignment

THREE—Radio call sign of the operations officer.

THREE CORPS—The military area around Saigon. Vietnam was divided into four corps areas.

TO&E—Table of Organization and Equipment. A detailed listing of all the men and equipment assigned to a unit.

TOC—Tactical Operations Center.

TOT—Time Over Target, referring to the time that aircraft were supposed to be over the drop zone with parachutists, or over the target if the planes were bombers.

TRICK CHIEF—NCOIC for a shift.

TRIPLE A—Antiaircraft artillery or AAA. Anything used to shoot at airplanes and helicopters.

TWO—Radio call sign of the intelligence officer.

TWO-OH-ONE(201) FILE—Military records file that listed a soldier's qualifications, training, experience and abilities. It was passed from unit to unit so that the new commander would have some idea about the capabilities of an incoming soldier.

UMZ—Ultramilitarized zone, the name GIs gave to the DMZ(Demilitarized Zone).

UNIFORM—Refers to UHF radio. Company Uniform the frequency assigned to that company.

USARV—United States Army, Vietnam.

VC—Vietcong, called Victor Charlie (phonetic alphabet) or just Charlie.

VIETCONG—Contraction of Vietnam Cong San (Vietnamese Communist).

VIETCONG SAN—Vietnamese Communist. A term in use since 1956.

WHITE MICE—Term referring to the South Vietnamese military police because they wore white helmets.

WIA—Wounded in Action.

WILLIE PETE—WP, white phosphorus, called smoke rounds. Also used as antipersonnel weapon.

WORLD—The United States.

WSO—Weapons System Officer. The name given to the man who rode in the back seat of a Phantom because he was responsible for the weapons systems.

XIN LOI—Vietnamese for "Sorry 'bout that."

XO—Executive officer of a unit.

ZAP—To ding, pop caps or shoot. To kill.

ZIP—Derogatory term applied to the South Vietnamese.

ZIPPO—Flamethrower.

A stark account of one of the Vietnam War's most controversial
defense actions.

VIETNAM: GROUND ZERO™

Shifting
FIRES

ERIC HELM

For seventy-seven days and nights six thousand Marines held the
remote plateau of Khe Sanh without adequate supplies or ammunition. As General Giap's twenty thousand troops move in to
bring the NVA one step closer to victory, an American Special
Forces squad makes a perilous jump into the mountainous Khe
Sanh territory in a desperate attempt to locate and destroy Giap's
command station.

**Nile Barrabas's most daring mission is
about to begin . . .**

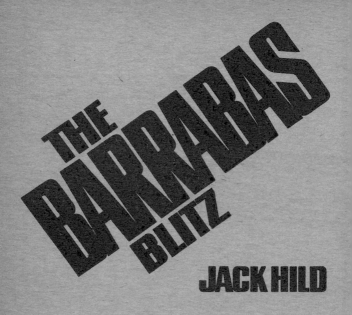

THE BARRABAS BLITZ

JACK HILD

*An explosive situation is turned over to a crack
commando squad led by Nile Barrabas when a
fanatical organization jeopardizes the NATO alliance
by fueling public unrest and implicating the United
States and Russia in a series of chemical spills.*

Mack Bolan's

PHOENIX FORCE

by Gar Wilson

The battle-hardened, five-man commando unit known as Phoenix Force continues its onslaught against the hard realities of global terrorism in an endless crusade for freedom, justice and the rights of the individual. Schooled in guerrilla warfare, equipped with the latest in lethal weapons, Phoenix Force's adventures have made them a legend in their own time. Phoenix Force is the free world's foreign legion!

"Gar Wilson is excellent! Raw action attacks the reader on every page."

—Don Pendleton

Mack Bolan's

ABLE TEAM

by Dick Stivers

Action writhes in the reader's own streets
as Able Team's Carl "Ironman" Lyons,
Pol Blancanales and Gadgets Schwarz
make triple trouble in blazing war. Join
Dick Stivers's Able Team as it returns to
the United States to become the country's
finest tactical neutralization squad in an
era of urban terror and unbridled crime.

"Able Team will go anywhere, do anything,
 in order to complete their mission. Plenty
 of action! Recommended!"
          —*West Coast Review of Books*

GOLD
EAGLE

Able Team titles are available
wherever paperbacks are sold.

AT-1